WORKING IN
MUSIC BUSIN___

GW00359300

WORKING IN THE MUSIC BUSINESS

RAY HAMMOND

BLANDFORD PRESS
POOLE · DORSET

First Published in the U.K. 1983 by Blandford Press,
Link House, West Street, Poole, Dorset BH15 1LL.

Distributed in the United States by
Sterling Publishing Co., Inc.,
2 Park Avenue, New York, N.Y. 10016.

ISBN 0 7137 1308 9 (hardback)
ISBN 0 7137 1413 1 (paperback)

Typeset in 11/13pt Paladium by Megaron Typesetting

Printed in Great Britain by Biddles Ltd., Guildford.

CONTENTS

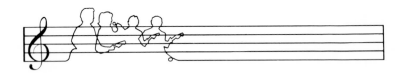

INTRODUCTION

During my years as Editor of various journals in the music business, I received thousands of letters from young people desperate to work in something — anything! — connected with music.

Many of these letter writers just wanted to find a way to meet their particular musical hero. Some were simply attracted by the 'glamour' of the business. Some were 'failed' musicians anxious to work with music and musicians.

All of these can be *good* reasons for wanting to be 'in the business'. Many successful music business people started their careers for similar reasons. The important fact to digest is that it is a *business*! Only the regular and properly balanced supply of money through any given company will ensure its survival and growth.

Many people seeking a career in the business have already had some peripheral contact. They might be forgiven for thinking that this is a business which tolerates idlers and 'liggers', and indeed these can be found in abundance. But these people are 'passing through' the industry. The record company office boy who dresses in the latest fashions and is on first name terms with the stars is a cliché. Equally the glamorous girl who works as a secretary for six months at a radio station and promptly marries a world-famous musician is the exception not the rule.

But there *is* glamour in the music business and, more importantly in the long run, there is the music. Only a career within show business (of which music is really just a part) can rival it for fun and fortune.

The shop assistant in a *music* shop in a provincial town is meeting *musicians* throughout the working day. The secretary in a theatrical agency has close contact with both artists and music. The sales representative from a musical wholesale company is likely to be selling to musicians — or ex-musicians. So the constant ingredient throughout the business is *music*.

If you love music (whatever type) there can be few businesses able to offer more fun than the music business. But there can be few businesses harder to get into. The music business is not an organised industry. There are no recognised channels of entry and there are no vocational training schemes (with one or two notable exceptions). If you want to work in the music business then read the following chapters and decide which branch interests you most. Try to talk to people already doing the job, to see if their experience agrees with your perception of the work. In each chapter I suggest some methods of approach — try them. Most importantly — go on trying them!

The key to success in the music business is to remember it is a *business*. Go to the parties, go to the concerts, but be sure you put something back into the business.

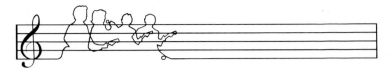

1

WORKING IN
SOUND RECORDING

Dear Sir,
  I am writing this letter because I want to work in a recording studio.
  I have always been interested in music and . . .

Such a letter *may* lead to an interview — but the writer would have to be very lucky for it to do so.

And yet the recording industry is bursting wide open, and there are more opportunities today than ever before. After 50 years as a 'closed shop', opportunities to enter the recording industry are opening up everywhere.

There are two main reasons for this. First, in the last decade, technology has improved recording equipment beyond recognition and has made it much cheaper. Second, the growth of local radio in Britain has opened up the field. Working in radio is rather different, but there are common aspects between sound recording and sound engineering for broadcast.

The recording industry is polarising. At one extreme the large, expensive recording studios are becoming even more expensive and prestigious. At the other extreme a small recording studio can be set up for £10,000 or less. Naturally there has been a huge growth in these small 'budget' studios and it is these which offer increased employment opportunities to a persistent applicant.

Traditionally there has been one main route to becoming a

balance engineer. It can best be summed up as being in the right place at the right time.

Balance engineers are the technicians who sit behind the huge consoles of knobs, sliders and buttons and mix the various sounds. The term 'balance' is a hang-over from the days when individual instruments had to be accurately balanced during recording. Today it is usual for each instrument, or group of instruments, to be recorded on individual tracks, allowing the engineer to concentrate on sound quality and then 'mix' the sounds at a later stage.

There are perhaps 20 really big recording studios in Britain. These have computerised equipment costing millions of pounds and naturally they are not prepared to place such equipment in the hands of an improperly-trained user.

Nearly all training for sound engineers is gained 'on the job'. There is one vocational training course for sound engineers run at the University of Guildford (details in the Appendix) and, not surprisingly, the competition for the annual eight places on the course is fierce, even though the course demands university entrance qualifications.

But the big studios still prefer to train their own engineers. Once trained, engineers do move from studio to studio, but the young novice intake is still the industry's favourite method of ensuring its future supply of trained technicians.

The system is simple, applicants are considered between the ages of 16 and 18 (if that's not you, read on, I'll get to you later). Any older and the studios consider that the trainees will require too much money, may have picked up pre-conceived ideas about sound recording or (more often the case) will make intimidating assistants for the 20-year-old senior balance engineers who have already had four years training. It's a business for young ears and after 30, most engineers have moved on and specialised in a particular branch of the industry such as record production or studio management.

Roger Cameron is Executive Director of Advision, one of London's most prestigious recording studios. He explains his

9

attitude to the employment of junior engineers.

'The ideal age for a young person entering a pop or rock music studio is when they've just left school, say 16 or 18. Hopefully, they will have got a number of 'O' levels.

'In recent years, examination results have become more important to studio managers. They consider an applicant's examination passes because they are an indication of intelligence. The gear in studios is a lot more sophisticated than it was and intelligence is an even more important prerequisite.

'Although the job was complex 20 years ago, there are now even more technical components in the recording chain — Dolbys, off-line equipment — and the concept is bigger to handle.

'Of course, there is one specialist course for engineers. It is the degree course offered by Surrey University — the Tonemeister degree course. A year of that course is spent trying to put the person out into industry, although in practice I would say that there are very few people who have actually gone through that particular degree course who have ended up as balance engineers. They're normally 22 or 23 by the time they graduate and in most cases they have tended to go directly into things like TV production, teaching, the BBC, etc.'

Despite the escalation in the demand for qualifications from applicants, each year every major studio receives hundreds of letters from young hopefuls, although even the biggest studio probably takes only two or three new trainee engineers a year. Clearly, the odds are not good for any applicant, and they're getting tougher.

Roger Cameron: 'When studios first started recording pop music, an employer would look for a very young, intelligent person with a lot of personality — the sort of person who could mix well socially and work easily with artists.

'That young person would have to be willing to work any number of hours that God sent for virtually no money. If he was keen enough, showed enterprise and also had a liking for music, he might have kept the job. But things have changed now. For example, although an understanding of music has always been useful for an engineer, today it is an added attraction if the applicant can read music. It is not vital, but it is very useful.

'These days there are several new factors that come into the studio job market. The general employment situation for young people is so poor that it means there are many young people seeking a job — any job! That means that the dedicated young person who yearns to become a sound engineer is competing against many people who really just want any job. It's up to the really keen person to prove he has got the ability.

'I get an average of two or three applications a day from young people who want to become balance engineers — a thousand a year. Put this against the fact that I have, on average, one vacancy every two years and the odds work out at two thousand to one against an individual application.

'For an applicant to be successful he must have some luck — he has to apply at the time I need someone, or to apply at the right time to another studio. Because there are so many applicants, I interview the people who look as though they have the best sort of academic background.'

Of course, it helps if you live (or are prepared to live) within easy reach of the studio — they're not all in London by the way. Recording is often done at very unsocial hours and the junior engineer who can't easily get a mini-cab home at three in the morning poses a headache.

Roger Cameron: 'I think that living locally is more of an important factor than it perhaps ought to be. It does have direct relevance to efficiency, however. Sessions often take place at odd hours and they do finish up at all times of day or night. It's usual that if a session finishes outside of normal hours, engineers are allowed to take a cab home — there aren't any buses at two in the morning. The studio will charge the cost of that cab on to the customer, but the cab fare has to be reasonable . . . you can't really have a guy living in Birmingham clocking up fifty quid in taxi fares.'

11

If you're in the right age bracket try and get some practical recording experience. This is easier than it sounds. Any musical instrument shop will tell you about 'budget' studios in your area and you might offer your services (unpaid) to a small studio just to get an idea of how the process is done (this will also give you a better idea of whether you *really* would be suitable for the work).

If there's no studio, or your offer of help is refused, go to the pubs and clubs (you probably need no urging) and meet some of your local bands. If you offer your services as a roadie you're unlikely to earn much more than an occasional drink (see the chapter about working on the road), but you will get into the recording studio when they do and in the meantime you'll learn a great deal about the technicalities of modern music production; experience which will stand you in good stead.

If both of the above ideas are impossible for you, try to get your hands on some recording equipment you can play with at home. A few pounds will secure an old 'reel to reel' tape machine, and with a single microphone and a few library books on sound recording, you will begin to learn something about the science.

Now that you live near (or have decided you are prepared to move to be near the studio if you get the job) and you are gaining some technical experience, how do you get the chance to show off your talents?

The key word in this chapter (and others) is *Persistence*.

You may write 100 letters to the big studios (several each, over a period of a few months) asking if there are any jobs for trainee engineers. All of them may result in rejection but the 101st may produce an invitation to an interview.

'Persistence is important,' agrees Cameron. 'If an applicant persists I will probably see him. Presentation of his letter is terribly important. It's something that in this country I feel that people tend to be very much less aware of than they are in the States. I have a feeling that in America the way in which a person makes himself presentable for a job is held to be very much more

12

Studio engineers in major studios are in command of extremely sophisticated equipment. This demands that the engineer has both artistic flair and a high level of technical skill — an unusual combination.

important. They're trained to do it properly in the US. If I get an application here from an American person who wants a job, their presentation is usually very much more professional. They always write a detailed account of themselves, accompanied by a *curriculum vitae* which lays out their academic background, etc . . . married/single, health, hobbies, other interests . . . it's all laid out well.

'Many of the letters that I get are appalling, but I consider presentation to be very important. If I get a very good letter and the person looks on paper to be bright, intelligent and he has the right sort of academic background, I might see the person even if I haven't got an immediate vacancy. If the person then proved to be interesting, I would follow it up when the time came.'

When you are writing to ask about vacancies take Roger Cameron's advice and *always* include relevant details — age, practical experience with sound equipment etc — and don't expect such details to be remembered from your first letter.

The qualifications considered necessary to work in the largest studios are spelled out by Roger Cameron.

'Apart from an obvious interest in music, an ability to read music is very useful and the person needs to have all of the other qualities that I mentioned before. In other words, the person has got to have that right type of personality. In some cases people sparkle during an interview, you know they're interesting people. So those things are just as important as they always were, but alongside that they need to have much more of an academic background that will enable them to understand the elements of high technology. The sort of things I tend to look for would be 'A' levels in maths and physics. One wouldn't necessarily look for someone who has a degree in electronics because apart from anything else that person would probably be 21 or 22 and therefore too old for entry.'

After writing your many letters, you must expect not to receive a reply from some studios. Others may send you a duplicated 'no vacancies' note. Don't despair after the first attempt but write to each studio once every three months addressing your applications to the studio manager. In your following letters state that you have written before, but make it clear that you are keener than ever to work for 'X' studio. If you faithfully apply, apply and apply again, the odds are that one of the letters will eventually cross a studio manager's desk at the time he is thinking about taking on a new trainee. If your age is

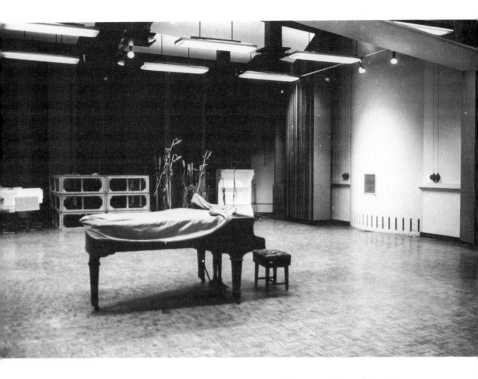

The CBS (London) recording studio waiting for a session. A junior engineer is expected to keep the studio looking as clean as this between sessions.

right and your experience or hobby is relevant he's likely to see you. It then depends on whether you are the right sort of person to work in the studio.

Regrettably, 99 per cent of sound engineers are male. But, as in everything else, discriminatory barriers are at last breaking down, and if you are female then your gender shouldn't stop you applying if you are sure sound engineering is for you.

'Yes, I think the business does discriminate against women,' says Cameron, 'but I don't think it's deliberate, as there is no particular reason why a woman couldn't physically do the job. Female engineers are common in broadcasting, in vision mixing

15

and areas like that. But in a music studio, particularly if the studio is orientated towards pop or rock, you're dealing with bands which tend to be predominantly made up of men. A lot of sessions take place through the evenings and night and inevitably having a female engineer creates a certain amount of tension, particularly if she's an attractive woman, and if she's attractive it is inevitable that somewhere down the line she's going to get into a romantic relationship with one of the musicians, or someone's going to make a pass at her which would inhibit the normal professional relationship between the people on the session. That is the main reason why rock engineers are male.'

If you are lucky enough to get an interview for a junior engineer's job, it will help if you can speak with some knowledge of sound recording techniques. (Although it is unwise to try to show off to the pros!)

Cameron: 'It is always a help if an applicant has had some experience with recording machinery, even the domestic kind. There was one guy we took on here who was initially working in a hi-fi shop. He saved his own money and paid for the two week concentrated engineers' course which is held at Surrey University each year — this is open to anyone — and he paid his money and got to play with the gear. The two week course can only concentrate on a few aspects of sound recording . . . microphone techniques and so on, but it has some value. This applicant had paid out his own cash, gone on to this course and by his own effort had showed he had initiative. We took him on.'

If you manage to find a job in a recording studio, you must be prepared to accept low wages in the beginning. Like so many interesting jobs, it seems that when you start you can have job satisfaction, or money, but not both together. In 1983 money, you'd get about £65 a week (one problem generated by this low wage is that it is very difficult for a non-local applicant to find sufficient cash for rented accommodation, especially in London). If that bothers you, however, you don't have the dedication to be a sound engineer. Roger Cameron describes Advision policy.

'In this particular studio we have had for many years a concept of payment to all of the people who are connected on session. This parameter would be the same for both the engineer and the assistant where they are paid a basic rate, a basic salary if you like and then an additional fee for each hour they work on a session which is charged to a client. Some years ago, when engineers were paid a salary plus overtime, it would often result in one particular engineer or assistant working with an artist who just happened to be working in the evening and on through the night and so they would be earning a salary plus overtime, while another engineer who might be working just as many hours but who would be working with an artist who was recording during the day, would only be earning a third of the other engineer's salary. At the end of a given year, a junior of 17 or 18 won't earn a great deal, maybe a total of three or three-and-a-half thousand.'

To some people in music, recording is the most boring, awful thing in the world. To others it's magic, a process of creating art (even if the session is for a dog-food jingle) through science: to those enthusiasts money matters far less than the idea of being involved in the production of music.

Let's assume you get a job as a trainee engineer in a big studio. (Believe me, you will if you want it enough!). Your position is likely to be described as either 'Trainee Engineer' or 'Junior Technical Engineer'. Either way, your first couple of weeks will be the same. You'll make coffee or tea, you'll be sent out to find hamburgers at midnight and you'll be a general dogsbody. If you suffer all this with a smile and spring willingly into action when asked, you'll get moved into the control room proper.

The control room is the heart of every recording studio. Here the main mixing console and the big tape recorders are situated. The balance engineer will sit at the console controlling the recording. Beside him will be the producer who is in overall charge.

17

Roger Cameron describes the duties which fall on the new recruit.

'He would have to assist the balance engineer who is respons-ible for the overall operation of that session. It could mean setting up for the session, setting up the microphones, putting the headphones out and checking that all the mikes and headphones are working. He will also have to load up the tape machines and make sure that they are running properly. In some studios the machines are still operated manually and in these studios the assistant will take on the rather old-fashioned role of tape operator, which means he controls the machines according to the engineer's instruction. In most modern studios the machines are now controlled remotely from the main desk. The assistant makes sure that the signal is going on to the machines during recording and he makes sure that everything is happening. He also has to attend to any of the needs of the engineer, the artists, the producer or anyone connected with the session.'

In big studios during major sessions, there may well be a first assistant engineer as well as a junior to assist the senior engineer. Most sessions, however, can be done with engineer and junior.

After the session the junior will have to clear up the studio. In the big studios you won't have to vacuum the floor, but you will have to remove and store all microphones and cable, clear all sound screens and generally get the studio ready for the next session. At four in the morning after 12 hours' recording this can seem an awful hardship but the junior wouldn't last long if the next engineers to use the studio found the mike cables tangled!

That's how you start. If you push the right buttons (and you will be overseen for at least six months) and you smile *whilst keeping your mouth shut* you will probably progress to some engineering tasks.

In the beginning, trainee engineers flex their muscles on previously recorded master tapes. During an hour or so, when one of the studios or mixing rooms is empty, the trainee will be allowed to put a non-vital 24-track tape on to the tape machine and attempt his or her own private mix. This teaches you precisely how the board works and allows you to experiment, and put into practice the techniques you have learned by observation over the hundreds of nights you have nursed your tape machines and set up microphones.

In the art of mixing there are no rules, only habits. Who is to say whether the drums are too loud? Who can say whether the lead vocal is high enough? In the commercial world the 'right' answer is the one that pleases most people, but in absolute terms, you can mix a track anyway you want.

This means that it takes talent to be a sound engineer. You can't learn the job in the way you can learn to spray-paint a car. Some people will never be able to make the right subjective judgements about sound and music, others will make them instinctively. If you passionately want to be a sound engineer you are already likely to have a degree of talent. But the proof only comes when you try. That part is in your hands.

So after a few private sessions, you get to engineer 'live' recordings and you have now become an 'Assistant Engineer'. By this time you know what needs to be done technically (which microphone to use for the bass drum, etc.) but you have no experience.

To start with you will be given non-essential sessions to record (for example, demos) and you will have an experienced sound engineer sitting beside you. You will also act as Assistant Engineer on big sessions, sometimes being given a section of the board, or of the orchestra, as your responsibility.

A recording engineer has great power. Even experienced musicians get nervous when they are recording and you will quickly discover whether you can instil the necessary confidence in the musicians you are recording. If the engineer copes with all their demands effortlessly and with a quiet smile, the musicians will ask for that engineer again. If he is a blur of arms and legs as he fumbles to trace an intermittent fault, they're going to be unsettled. Bringing order to chaos is part of an engineer's role and the person who panics, loses.

19

Sound recording has become a high-tech job. This mixing desk at London's Advision studios is computer controlled and demands a

high degree of both technical and artistic skill from the sound engineer.

Music-making is an intensely personal operation. When a potential hit record is being made the atmosphere in the studio is electric. Every member of the team is willing the embryo recording to grow to greater and greater strength and, like any birth, only the family and the doctor (the engineers), are welcome. This is why a personality which is at ease with people is a vital quality in an engineer.

As a trainee engineer proper you will be doing your own small sessions while assisting on larger recordings. You may still be required to play the role of humble junior on occasion, but sometimes you will be second engineer on a big mix, assisting a senior engineer in a complicated reduction.

After a couple of years you will be regarded as a balance engineer in all but name and pay packet. You'll have to do another few years before the title 'senior engineer' and appropriate financial reward comes your way, but you should be having a great time.

Don't think of becoming a sound engineer if you want a busy social life. It's impossible! A typical working week (for a junior or a senior engineer) might be:

Monday, day off.
Tuesday, get to the studio at noon to prepare the studio for session. Start recording at 3p.m. Finish recording at 3a.m. Clear the studio up and get home by 5a.m.
Wednesday, back in the studio by 11a.m. after only three hours sleep. Record until midnight.
Thursday, day off.
Friday, in studio by 8a.m. Morning session till 1p.m. Break until 5p.m. Prepare studio for major session starting at 8p.m. Recording until 8a.m.
Saturday, sleep until 2.30p.m. Get to the studio by 4p.m. Prepare for continuation of previous night's session. Record until 8a.m.
Sunday, grab a few hours sleep. Record through the night again. Which is why you may get Monday off — if there's nothing urgent to do.

It's a punishing schedule and if your love of music is merely a mad whim it will melt away — like ice cream in an oven — under the heat of constant exposure to music and long, underpaid hours. However, if the music's in you, you'd never willingly do anything else!

That's life in one of the big studios. It's rather different in a small studio.

I said at the beginning of the chapter that a polarisation is occurring between the big studios and the 'budget' establishments. The main reason is technology.

Ten years ago a big studio would offer either 8 or 16 tracks of simultaneous recording power. The big tape machines then cost about £15,000. Today a good 8-track machine can be bought for £2,500. Multi-track recording has become available to many more people.

But as the cost of basic recording equipment has fallen, so the sophistication of 'high end' technology has increased. Every big studio today uses computers to control mix-down. This allows engineers to programme a computer to remember their moves during a mix so that the engineers are not continuously forced to make the thousands of alterations to echo, tone equalisation or sound balance necessary during a 24 or 48 track mix.

Also, tape recorders are on the way out. Before long they will have been replaced by 'digital' recording equipment. Instead of recording sounds onto a tape, this equipment stores the sounds in a computer memory, allowing far greater control and quality.

To equip a large studio with a computerised mixing console and digital recorder can easily cost a million pounds. Added to that is the cost of the premises — often purpose-built. So you'll realise that a studio of this type is a major investment.

But, at the other end of the scale, a local businessman can now equip a perfectly adequate small studio for less than £10,000. Premises are likely to be a converted basement or church hall, but the results should be quite satisfactory. These budget studios (usually 8 or 16 track maximum) are quite capable of turning out high quality masters as well as excellent demos. It may properly

23

be asked why any musician, however famous, will spend £150 per hour on studio time when quite acceptable recordings can be made for £30 an hour.

The answer is in the very nature of the business and is too long and too complicated to be discussed here. It is certain, however, that successful musicians will continue to spend ten times as much money making a recording which is only ten per cent better. To them that ten per cent is vital, and as digital recording becomes the norm, tape machines will be relegated to demo use.

You may not be between 16 and 20 but you may still wish to get into sound recording. If the foregoing makes you want to cut your throat or apply for a pension — don't. There are other ways for older applicants to get in. The small studios care less about the age of their employees. I don't imagine that many would be prepared to take on a 45-year-old sheet metal worker who has been made redundant, but there are not the same ground rules here as in the big studios. Unfortunately, the training is not as good either.

Some small studios are highly professional. These are probably owned and run by ex big-studio engineers who have opted for their own business and here the novice can expect a high standard of training. Some studios, however, have been built by people with little experience. Some are enthusiastic amateurs while some are businessmen who sense a quick killing to be made, and in these situations the novice has to be very good at picking things up for himself.

The proliferation of small studios means that you are likely to live in reasonable striking distance of one without having to move. The problem is to know where they are. Ask in your local musical instrument shops — they will undoubtedly know of some. Subscribe to the UK magazines I have listed at the end of this book (you would also do well to get the US magazines, they're more up-to-date technically and carry a great deal of information). In the magazines you will see ads for the smaller studios and you will eventually get a list of all the outfits you can apply to. Regretfully, the Job Centres are very unlikely ever to

*The advent of 'budget recording' has encouraged many small
studios to open. This one has been built into a house (with the
Edwardian fireplace still visible). Although still fitted with
sophisticated equipment, small out-of-town studios such as this can
provide training and experience for applicants who might not find a
place in the major studios.*

have an opening for a sound engineer without experience.

Small studios have no organised training scheme, but once in
a blue moon they need extra help. Because the recording
business is so attractive there is never a shortage of willing
novices asking for jobs so it's up to you to make your application
specially attractive.

The same ground rules apply here as for the larger studios.

25

Any experience at all is a help. If you've been acting as a road manager for a local band you will get to know some of the studios and diligent 'hanging out' will not only teach you a great deal, it may also provide an opening.

You must be prepared to work for less than you would expect to get in other jobs and you must be prepared to work very unsocial hours.

A small studio will put you in the driving seat very rapidly. Within a matter of weeks of arriving you will either be engineering or looking for another job. You will learn the job under pressure and you'll often be finding out how to work a piece of equipment whilst a session is underway. Here, once again, the most important personal quality is a cool head and a pleasant smile. You will obviously be shown how things work, but your ability to teach yourself will be a major asset. You will have to read every book and magazine which even touches on recording and you will discover one important aspect which wouldn't really concern a balance engineer in a bigger studio — maintenance!

In large studios there are balance engineers and maintenance engineers and they are worlds apart. The maintenance engineer services the equipment and fixes it when it breaks down. By the nature of the equipment, it's a highly- skilled job and although the engineer is working in a musical environment, he or she is an *electronics* engineer, who might just as easily be servicing missile guidance systems.

In small studios the subject of maintenance is much closer to the balance engineer. In all but the 'one man band' operations, balance engineers aren't expected to whip out an oscilloscope and test some component in a printed circuit, but they are expected to have a theoretical appreciation of how the equipment works. In the middle of a session you might choose to send a vocal signal to an echo unit. If echo is not forthcoming you

It doesn't cost a great deal to set up a small multi-track studio today. This Allen and Heath/Brenell set-up is typical of the inexpensive yet efficient systems now available.

need to know the system to investigate why. It may be that you haven't patched (linked) the system up properly. It may be that a connection is broken. In a small studio the engineer is expected to check on these things and will often be expected to re-solder a plug onto a cable. If the echo unit itself is faulty, he will be expected to remove it from the circuit and establish another echo source. In a big studio the procedure on breakdown used to be to lift the telephone and in a cultured voice request the attendance of one of the maintenance staff. These days, balance engineers have an increasing technical awareness and they are likely to be able to diagnose which part has gone wrong.

Most engineers working in small studios dream about working in big studios. Most are too old to stand a chance of becoming a 'trainee' and they haven't gained the experience of computerised consoles and digital recording machines necessary to establish themselves in the big league. Most feel they will forever be confined to small studios — but that need not be the case. By study, by making friends with other engineers and by visiting technical exhibitions (such as the annual London show promoted by the Association of Professional Recording Studios — address in appendix) they may gain an appreciation of the more sophisticated equipment, which can open the necessary doors.

Very often, engineers will form friendships with musicians they record, sometimes developing to a point where musicians will record with no one else. This development leads to a further category of engineers — the 'independent'.

The independent engineer may have trained at either a small or large studio. By one means or another he has impressed a group of clients sufficiently for them always to ask for him. A few years ago, large studios relied on the talent of their engineers to draw clients back to that studio, but a sort of engineers' lib has resulted in these favoured people leaving the studio and relying on clients to purchase their services directly.

The independent engineer has to be the master of a great deal of technical equipment. If a superstar decides to record in

*Recording engineers aren't always tied to one location. Mobile
recording has become popular and this articulated truck transports
a complete studio to any location in Europe.*

The inside of the Mobile One studio. Although the equipment is contained in a single truck, note the twin 24-track machines and sophisticated mixing consoles.

Jamaica, the engineer flown out will have to be able to use unfamiliar equipment. Sometimes the engineer will have to record in live situations, such as concerts, and will often have to follow principal clients around the world.

After a spell in a recording studio, during which most engineers will undertake a wide variety of work, many choose to specialise and concentrate on a particular branch of music or recording. Roger Cameron explains what happens.

'What route an experienced engineer chooses to follow obviously depends to a certain extent on the type of studio that person is employed in. If it is essentially a rock or pop studio that would be the type of material he would be orientated towards. If it is a much more flexible studio, perhaps like EMI, the choice is wider. It may be that he starts to concentrate on sessions for advertising, which is a very specialised area, and the techniques are slightly different. In advertising, speed and efficiency are more important than anything else.

'But even if an engineer does specialise, being a studio engineer can be quite a short career. It is not so true for people who are involved in classical recording, nor is it true for people who are recording in advertising or film. If you're recording music for film scores, for example, you can continue to quite a reasonable age, perhaps 55 or so.

'For a pop engineer the length of his career depends on how long he can go on relating to the current music. Once a new generation arrives with a new fashion, I think that person has got to do something else. He's got to move on to studio management, record production or into another type of music. He may be clever enough to be able to encompass his knowledge over a new generation's music, like Martin Rushent has in his productions with the Human League, etc, but the actual span of time he can remain a balance engineer in pop is limited. It is probably a ten year career.'

With the arrival of the microcomputer, many changes are occurring in the recording studio. This is one reason why Roger

Cameron and other studio directors now demand more than just an easy-going personality from recruits.

'Recording is going to become much more akin to a computer operation. Years back, perhaps even today, the concept of a balance engineer needing to type would seem ludicrous, but in the coming days of complex computer programming such abilities are going to become much more important. The ability to input data becomes as important as the ability to mix.

'In some ways engineering is becoming less of an artistic job and more of a scientific occupation, although there is still some artistry and some creativity required.'

Roger Cameron's advice to young hopefuls is not inspiring.

'My advice to young people who want to go into recording would be . . . don't. It depends whether one is looking at it from a long or short term viewpoint. Historically, there are many people who have gone into the industry as balance engineers and who have ended up at 30 incapable of doing anything at all. I suppose it is the same sort of thing as being a pop musician — if the person is not capable of moving on to something else he's had it.

'So I would say, don't — unless you feel really desperate about it. If you do, then there's no reason why it can't be a very enjoyable job, providing you look at the whole aspect of the career. Try to remember that you've got to think about your career's progression for the time when you are finished with that particular era of music. Try to think about the possibilities you could move on to . . . owning your own studio, whatever.'

33

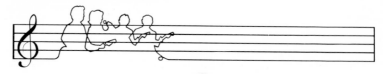

2
WORKING IN A RECORD COMPANY

Between 1950 and 1975 there were only six major record companies and 20 or so independent labels. Today there are thousands of independent labels, most of them distributed by the same six major record companies. The shift caused by the emergence of the more independent 'punk' generation, has been a creative shift rather than a complete change in trading patterns.

Joining a record company is something thousands of school and college leavers dream about, many of them cherishing the illusion that life inside such an organisation is one long round of chatting to superstars and arranging TV appearances. The truth is rather different.

Very few small independent labels can afford to employ anybody who is not directly involved in music-making. If secretarial help is needed, it is likely to be provided by a 'friend' on a part-time basis rather than by a full-time, properly trained secretary.

The large record companies — EMI, CBS, Polydor, Philips, Decca, etc. — keep a substantial administrative and creative staff and there are many opportunities here — although every job advertised is almost instantly oversubscribed.

There are five main areas of work within a record company and you must analyse why you want to work in a record company before you decide which is the most suitable for you.

It is quite legitimate to want to work in a record company because you love music, but you will have to accept the fact that much work undertaken by a record company appears to have little direct association with music and the occasional periods of direct contact will have to be savoured purely because they are very occasional.

The areas in a record company which might prove attractive (and accessible) to a school or college leaver are as follows: secretarial and administrative, sales, production, promotion and A&R. The last category is usually known as production, but I have used the antiquated, but perhaps more accurate term A&R (artists and repertoire) to separate it from the 'mechanical' production department which oversees such operations as record pressing and sleeve printing.

You *can* join a record company as a secretary and end up as a star. Martha (of the 1960s girl-group Martha and the Vandellas) was one of the first to do so and Hazel O'Connor is one of the most recent.

Record companies know they're on to a good thing when it comes to employing impressionable young men and women, and so they often offer junior administrative jobs at appallingly low wages — you'd get more behind a counter in Woolworths. You have to decide whether you want the fun or the money.

The duties in a secretarial role depend on the record company, the department you're in and the whims of your boss. Secretaries in the A&R department write to artists, arrange travel for executives and artists, talk to managers and agents, ward off the thousands of hopefuls who besiege the offices and learn to say, 'he (or she) isn't available this afternoon.'

If you want to be a singer, you're closer to where it happens in the A&R department than anywhere else. Secretarial jobs are like gold dust, go almost exclusively to women and, sadly and most unfairly, go to the pretty ones more often than the law of averages should dictate.

The promotion departments (also called the plugging department in old-fashioned jargon) are the next most exciting places to be. These departments house the footsore hustlers who have to stalk the corridors of radio and TV stations, waiting to pounce on producers or DJs and force-feed them their latest 'product'. (If you get into a record company you'll have to get used to the fact that no one refers to it as music, it's always the 'product'.)

People capable of braving the slings and arrows of outrageous rudeness suffered when hustling new records generally make bad bosses. They're cocky, overconfident and insensitive. They have to be, to go on doing their thankless task. But they're fun; the adrenalin level is high and if you join a promotion department you'll find yourselves phoning producers, DJs, artists, managers, agents and almost every other type of individual or organisation in the business. You're more likely to end up as a record plugger yourself than a singing star.

One department I didn't list, but which flourishes inside most record companies, is the publicity department. This is usually staffed with ex-journalists and the chapters on *The Music Media* and *The Fringes* offer detailed advice about entering the music business by this route. Publicity departments do, however, employ secretaries and helpers and if you work here you will be filing, writing to media people and arranging interview schedules for visiting artists. People in the publicity department do come into close contact with the recording artists.

Secretarial duties in the mechanical production department of a record company tend to be mundane. Orders for a pressing of records have to be completed in triplicate, artwork for record labels and sleeves has to be checked and double checked and lengthy cost sheets filled in. Only rarely do workers get the chance to come into contact with artists, but it is agreeable work and probably better than a similar job in a shoe factory.

The major record companies all have two divisions; creative and sales. The head office is always the creative office situated in a classy part of the city, whilst the sales part usually occupies a huge factory space on a trading estate by an orbital road. Working in a secretarial capacity at the sales end of a record company you may as well be working for a shipping line. You'll only get the most occasional whiff of greasepaint, and most of your time will be spent writing letters about the number of shipments dispatched to Nigeria.

If you are sufficiently qualified to hope to enter a record company at a high level, you must be even more positive about what you want to do and why. Like any desirable job, there are always more applicants than positions and before you go to make out your case for employment to an interviewer, it is a wise thing to make the case out thoroughly in your own mind. Below, I list the type of opportunities which exist, but you will have to work out why you might be particularly suited for any individual department.

The dream of being a record producer is one that is cherished in many hearts, but the major record companies gave up employing inexperienced 'A&R men' in the middle 1960s. There are very few 'staff' record producers today, as almost every producer who has made a hit, demands the right to go it alone and become an independent. Despite this, several of the largest record companies still keep staff producers whose sole job it is to find new talent, groom it, find the right material for recording and produce a record which will be an instant hit — at least, that is the theory.

It is very hard to make a hit record. If that sounds like a truism, ask yourself if you've ever spotted a hit before it made the charts. Most of us believe we have — and this leads to the temptation of thinking that if we can spot a hit from the finished product, surely we can produce hits ourselves — which isn't necessarily the case. I discovered this when I became a record producer in 1969. In retrospect, I consider producing to be an appalling job. The fun parts are acting the role of big shot and signing up artists. The unbearable parts are sitting through hours of repetitive recording, trying to hold an image of a particular sound in your mind, whilst being distracted by fatigue, boredom, broken guitar strings, stroppy session musicians and sexy ladies (or men). Even if you manage to create the sound you

The author as record producer — pictured at Pye circa 1969.

started out aiming for, it is a supreme act of ego to assume that it will be commercial, and only the most dedicated and ruthless producers discover the knack of producing hit after hit. When that is discovered, it is invaluable and in my opinion the hit producers, Martin Rushent, Trevor Horne, etc, deserve every penny of the millions they earn.

There are no formal qualifications required to become a

The author in his own 'budget' studio — 1983

record producer: it's talent that is required. You *can* start out on your own as a producer. You need to learn about recording studios, recording techniques, record pressing techniques, music, instruments and (most of all) people. You will need to put your money where your mouth is and fork out for a session at a cheap out-of-town recording studio. This is costing less and less in real money, as there is now a proliferation of budget studios

39

(many trading unprofitably) around the country. Find a good act, talk them into letting you produce a couple of tracks (and giving you an option to produce more), rehearse them until you're blue in the face, hire the studio and take them in. The problem for most young would-be producers is that they have no real yard-stick against which to judge talent. The 'Big Shots' who sit in their leather swivel chairs have, over the years, listened to thousands of live performances and tens of thousands of demo records. When they judge an act, they are judging it against their wealth of experience, but, if you're young and inexperienced, you've either got to have a superb ear or you've got to be very lucky.

There are no rules in record production. Phil Spector made incredible records by bending the will of the musicians and singers to his own and creating wonderful musical monstrosities. Joe Boyd (Fairport Convention and many others) made records by seemingly making the studio and engineers invisible and capturing the most truthful rendition possible of an artist's performance. The right way is the way that works.

Having made a record you have to turn yourself into a sales-person and sell it to a label. That takes endless letters, phone calls and visits. Even if you can't sell it, you may have impressed someone with either the act or your production. Make it clear in every occasion that you're an independent producer on the look-out for good acts because no producer can be better than the artists he or she takes into the studio (perhaps Spector was the exception that proved the rule). If you hustle hard enough, if you have an instinctive ability at production and if you're a nice person, you may persuade a large record company to give you a new act they've signed to make a record — they certainly won't give you a staff job these days. Becoming an independent record producer is rather like being a musician: you've got to be prepared to starve.

The second greatest quality needed in a record producer is the ability to concentrate (after the ability/experience to spot a hit in the raw stages). Once you've rehearsed the act and got them into the studio, it is concentration and will-power which forces you to go on until you get the right product. If you allow anything to divert you from your end goal, the record will be weakened.

If you fancy yourself as a song plugger and you've got what it takes to be successful, you will find it easy to get a job with any of the major record companies. The reason being that the cheek needed to talk yourself into a plugging department is nothing to the cheek needed to start out plugging records. The old hands at the game know everybody — or at least appear to. They're on first name terms with this producer and that DJ and they often spend weekends on luxury yachts with radio station controllers. They are all parasites (many are likeable parasites) and they live in mortal dread of the time when the welcoming smile turns to an irritated frown.

If you can talk your way into a promotion department you will be given a batch of the least attractive new releases, pointed in the direction of an irrelevant radio station in some dispirited part of the country and told to 'get plays'. To do this you have to leap over the windowsills of producers and talk at them until they agree to play one of your wretched records just to get rid of you (the trick is at all times to appear so nice that you don't raise a hostile response). The same course of action must be taken against the DJ, only here you have to be even nicer because the DJ can be nasty about your product on the air. It works well if you can play the producer and DJ off against each other. 'Rob said he loved this . . . he just wants your OK to put it on tomorrow's One O'clock Show.' You've got to be fast on your feet to whip round to Rob's office to convince him that his producer is dying for it before they can make a phone connection and discover your trick.

Many radio stations and broadcasting bodies try to insist that they have an official 'play list' of records and that pluggers are wasting their time trying to promote records that don't appear on this list, but the plain fact is that on many radio stations, producers have power to include any record they choose and the

41

successful pluggers are continually evading the smokescreen of the playlist. The BBC recognised this some time ago and scrapped the idea of the playlist.

Payola (pay off) does exist in broadcasting, the stakes are too high for it not to — but there is very little direct bribery. Most pluggers choose to buy their favours with a few drinks at the bar rather than crinkled pound notes — their ego demands that they should have talked the producer into playing the record, rather than having to buy it.

Television is much harder work for song pluggers. There are very few regular pop music programmes and those that do go out each week are formally structured to avoid the possibility of bribery (after a scandal a few years back!). Most pluggers restrict their activities to radio stations and only the most senior are allowed to hammer TV producers over the head.

Working in the mechanical production end of a record company can lead to interesting things. Some production departments have design studios attached and, depending on your own leanings, avenues of progress may open to design, recording (see previous chapter) and even record production. The work itself is monotonous but demanding. If there's a mis-spelled word in the sleeve copy of a famous artist's latest album it will always be there because of the failure of the production department. If records aren't available from the factory when they are needed, the factory will most certainly blame the production department. The production department may be closely linked with the design side of the publicity department and this cross-over can add interest to an otherwise boring job.

The one area that many hopefuls overlook is record sales, yet many ex- salesmen (no women as yet) now grace the board-rooms of the major record companies. There are fewer travelling record salesmen than there were ten years ago and a great deal of selling is done over the telephone, but if you like travelling and have what it takes to become a sales rep — and you enjoy music — you should look in the back of journals such as *Music and Video Week* and try to persuade a sales manager to take you on.

If you're a salesperson, you will be working from the unglamorous end of the business — the warehouse on the trading estate. You will normally be provided with an estate car (there are very few van salespeople left) and you will head off to make your weekly calls on the few small record shops that are still trading. Many have been forced out of business by the fierce discount war which dominated record retailing in the 1970s and the multiple stores order centrally by phone.

One advantage that the salesperson has over all others in the record company, is that he or she actually finds out what the record business is like at the sharp end — where the records are bought. Salespeople can make a hit on their own — just by promoting it strongly to retailers: retailers will always try and sell what they've got in stock. It's a wise artist who offers a gold watch to the salesperson who achieves the best performance with his or her latest product.

The salesperson has also become closely involved in the 'hyping' process. Direct bribery has waned over the last ten years as repeated investigations into payola have revealed sorry scapegoats, who have then unfairly borne the brunt of an industry's conspiracy. Rather than pay producers and DJs to play records, record companies now prefer to hype the charts from the dealer end. In an effort to beat this, the BBC keeps changing its method of chart compilation but they can't deny the fact that a record is selling. The fact that it may be selling for corrupt reasons, is outside their control.

The system works by giving record dealers inducements to stock certain records. The most common inducement is to give the particular records free to selected dealers, or supply them at greatly reduced cost, and with the incentive of a whacking 100% profit margin the record company can rely on the dealer to bring the record forcibly to the attention of his regular customers and the local club DJs who rely on him to keep them informed. Many dealers often sell these records as a 'blackmarket extra' and the cash never appears on their books, in effect, doubling their profitability.

This type of hype is cheap for the record companies — if they give away 5,000 singles, they'll be sure of selling a minimum of 25,000 if the record takes off — and it ensures that dealers will make a genuine effort to promote the record. As a result, these dealers can truthfully report high sales of that particular record and their customers can truthfully report having purchased them. Even quite sophisticated poll techniques can't argue with a fan who has purchased a record. The difficulty lies in identifying the dealers and regions which will be used for chart compilation, but with so much hanging on gaining an entry to the Top 40, it's not surprising that one way or another it is always discovered. Even without the tip-offs, the retail network has shrunk to such an extent that even a haphazard hype is likely to produce a result.

If it shocks you to learn that almost every new name that enters the charts does so as a result of underhand hype, you are not really ready to enter the music business. You can comfort yourself in the knowledge that even hyped artists can't sustain success without talent. Dealer hype is now regarded as being one of the more legitimate methods of promoting records.

The record business is in a bad way. Only a quarter of the number of records are now being sold, by the traditional method (through retail outlets), compared with ten years ago, but the number of people trying to make hits has increased a hundred-fold. The result is that record companies are no longer the havens for lounging, fashionable youth they once were. The days when school leavers were kept on the staff specifically to look pretty or to run errands has long gone.

If you join a record company today, in almost any capacity, you will work harder and earn less than in almost any other occupation. For those with the right qualities, working in the record business can be a life-long career and a highly rewarding one — emotionally as well as financially — but it is one of the most demanding areas of the business.

44

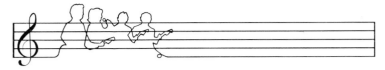

3

WORKING IN
THE MUSIC MEDIA

Each year, thousands of young people leave education with a desire to work 'in the music business'. Thousands more want to be 'in the media' and many would like to be in both. These twin aims combine to ensure that when a vacancy occurs in a radio station, or in the editorial department of a paper like *Sound, Smash Hits* or *International Musician* the ratio of applicants to opportunities is so high that it would be hysterically funny if it weren't so sad.

During the 1970s, when I was regularly employing journalists in the music press, there were approximately 150 applicants for every post. Today my friends who are still working in the music press tell me that they're almost frightened to advertise a vacancy as they are sure to be deluged with sackfuls of mail and besieged by phone calls.

The pressure has become so great that unsolicited letters often provide editors with potential applicants long before a vacancy occurs, and, as a result, the job ad never appears.

'Doing something in the media' seems to be the most popular choice for school and college leavers with an ability in English. For every journalistic, or quasi journalistic job which is available there is a massive flood of applications, many from people vastly overqualified.

Having said that, if you want to get into radio or into the music press badly enough, you will! There is an old maxim in journalism that it is impossible to get into and only those who can achieve the impossible are suitable to be journalists. There may be some truth in that, but I have watched many people get in by luck, others by dogged determination and a few by accident (sometimes unwillingly). You get a job in the music media by having two things: the necessary skills and the determination to go on asking.

Before discussing the necessary skills, it is important to point out that working in the music media is working in a 'no man's land' that lies somewhere between working in the music business and working in the media. Some would consider that it offers the worst of both worlds — and it is true that music scribes and DJs are disliked and feared by musicians and spurned by their more conventional 'hard news' journalistic colleagues. Others consider it offers the best of choices, allowing a person who loves both writing or broadcasting and music to combine his or her passions into one glorious (but often short) career.

The qualifications necessary to land a job as a music journalist are usually considered to include formal journalistic training and a thorough knowledge of the current music scene. Unlike most aspects of the music business, there are many training courses in journalism available which will be of use to the hopeful applicant trying to get into the music press. All of these courses are concerned with mainstream journalism rather than the music business, but a qualification from such a course will certainly make you a more attractive applicant than someone without the training.

There are several branches of the music press. The better-known papers are, in the main, owned by large companies and they insist that all journalists have received both training and experience. Some of the smaller publications, especially the monthly magazines, are more flexible in their requirements, but nobody is going to give a journalistic job to somebody who has no training and no experience.

The National Council for the Training of Journalists lays down the formal requirements for qualification as a journalist.

The traditional path of entry is to join a local newspaper as a junior reporter, serve a probationary period of six months and then sign 'indentures' for a further two-and-a-half year's training.

Such a formal structure shouldn't put you off, even if all you want to do is write about music. Within six weeks of joining a London local paper in 1966 I was writing *Pop Notes* every week and I found I managed to wangle things so that I was writing about music or show business almost exclusively. (The editor did finally lose patience with my lack of interest in 'hard news' and I was fired nine months later.)

The minimum qualifications necessary to gain entry to local newspaper journalism are (theoretically) six O-levels or equivalent. In practice, the shortage of jobs has pushed this up to six Os and two As (with English always the first requirement). Training in shorthand and typing is given on the job, although an applicant with either skill will often be selected in preference to someone who has to start from scratch.

If you don't have the necessary qualifications, don't despair, there is a very large back door into journalism, and especially into music journalism. Forget about the local papers and concentrate on magazines. I don't just mean the magazines you will find on the news stand — I include the thousands of 'trade' publications with exotic titles such as *The Muck Shifter* (one of my favourites) and *Glass Blower's World*.

Magazines are not nearly as strict about entry qualifications as local newspapers. The minimum qualification for these journals is a clutch of O-levels — always including a good grade in English — and if you manage to clamber on board either a consumer or trade publication you will receive 'training by experience'. I tolerated life on the *Off Licence Journal* for six months once, while I was managing pop groups by night, and although the subject matter of such publications can be tedious, the job usually allows sufficient freedom to be able to escape unnoticed for an afternoon. After a year or two on such a publication you are ready to bombard the estalished music press

*The typical ad lib interview. Here Rick Wakeman and girlfriend
Nina Carter are interviewed by a radio interviewer during a London
music show. The key qualities for an interviewer are a fast mind and
a slick tongue, but although some interviewees are tolerant of ill-
prepared reporters (especially Rick) most give the brash know-
nothing questioner a very hard time.*

with requests for an interview and now you have practical experience in journalism to offer. With that, your chances improve considerably, and now depend on how much you know about fashionable music (it's no good loving only 1950s stuff) and how well your face fits (always an imponderable).

If you haven't *any* qualifications, you need more than a little luck. Music magazines and newspapers occasionally advertise for 'persons Friday' or editorial assistants. If you're a Friday you play the role of 'gofer' and you go for anything the writers want. You will file photographs, make phone calls, accept abuse and always smile (if you want to stay). Occasionally you will have an album tossed in your direction; you might also get the odd set of concert tickets and you will have a lot of fun. If you keep your mouth shut, your eyes open and bide your time, there is a fair chance you will eventually be thrown the editorial jobs that nobody else wants. Seize them as though they were an exclusive interview with your particular idol and do them thoroughly and conscientiously. These tasks include such jobs as compiling lists of coming events and running readers' letters columns. It is quite likely that you will finally join the main editorial team, although in my experience you only become fully accepted in your new role when you move to a different publication on which your shameful, untrained background isn't remembered. I have watched at least half-a-dozen people rise from the 'other ranks' in this way.

Patience, persistence and niceness seem to be the common factors among music writers and the experience such people bring to their job often has more practical use than the formal training offered on newspapers.

An ex-colleague of mine started work at 15 as a filing clerk in a newspaper office in Fleet Street, switched to being a Friday on *Melody Maker* and moved to undertake the same function on *Sounds* when it was formed as a break-away publication. He eventually became assistant editor on that paper and ended up as editor of *Record Mirror*. Today he is running his own editorial consultancy, producing music publications for a variety of publishers.

49

Editorial assistants are one step up from Fridays. A qualification in English is usually an essential requirement, but the successful applicant is still likely to find him or herself fetching and carrying, although a part of their work will have an editorial content.

Whatever route of entry seems right for you, there is one common quality which will be necessary: persistence. I have already pointed out that all vacancies are totally oversubscribed and in this type of market-place it is not always the most qualified who shine out. This may seem odd, but human nature decrees that editors won't wade through 300 applications to check whether a late applicant has a better English degree or has six months' additional experience. The editor seizes on the first few good letters he or she sees and interviews the applicants.

If we take it as read that applicants for a journalistic job have an English examination pass plus some experience on a newspaper or magazine, I would say that the two things that will be deciding factors will be persistence and writing style.

If you want to work in the music press, tell the editors you do and keep on telling them. You will not offend an editor if you write every three months politely enquiring about a vacancy. You should not be offended if you do not get a reply; some editorial offices are sufficiently well organised for replies to be sent out, others are not. Even if you hear nothing from an editor, you should keep reminding him or her of who you are. If you are considered unsuitable you will eventually be told, but your main task should be to make yourself suitable. You may notice that editorial names are changing on the paper's masthead even as you are writing your endless letters: do not despair! Vacancies are often pre-filled for a year ahead. It will take persistence to force your correspondence to stand out above the regular piles of begging letters that arrive.

There is a standard form of application letter that is suitable for sending to music papers, but within the format there is scope for individuality. Every application letter should be neatly typed (handwriting just won't do) and it should be accompanied by a separate *curriculum vitae* clearly listing your background. Do try and get access to a word-processor. Writing endless application letters is time consuming and it also becomes dispiriting as the eventual rejections arrive. If you have been unemployed for some time, you may (understandably) have begun to feel paranoid about your chances of ever finding work. Getting application letters automated on a word-processor is an enormous fillip: and even if it means going back to school and borrowing one, or finding the small amounts of money necessary to have a standard letter of application plus CV held by a word-processing bureau, you will find that it completely alters your attitude to letter writing and what was an awful chore becomes a pleasure.

What you write is, of course, more important than the method you use to write it. Below I reproduce two letters I received during my years as an editor. They are completely different, but they both succeeded in grabbing my attention.

September 1975

Dear Sir,
There is a limit to every man's patience, including mine!
Thin Lizzie are using 10K of front-line amplification on their current tour. This is, no doubt, a source of great pleasure to both Phil and the boys and to the fans. Last night, however, it was a source of great annoyance to me.
The Conservative councillor for Hamilton Park Ward (West) was advancing particularly cogent reasons why work on a new sewer should be delayed for a month at a meeting of the engineer's sub-committee of the Sutton Borough Council. Having been sent by my Editor (*Sutton Advertiser*, circulation 32,000, Fridays) to reveal the power politics that wrack the backroom decision-making of Sutton's elders, I was naturally annoyed to discover that the small, dusty room used for committee meetings was immediately adjacent to the Town Hall. As soon as Phil hit a bottom E to open the show, business

51

came to an end in the committee room. For a moment it seemed as though Councillor Holland had been struck dumb. His mouth opened and closed, but neither I, nor the committee members were able to hear his words.

Having spent a week toadying to our ageing-queen of a show business editor for the two review tickets for the Lizzie concert (which so clearly were of no interest to him), imagine my annoyance when, having resigned myself to probing the graft-ridden world of sewer replacement, I found the meeting postponed (later to waste yet another evening) and my appetite whetted but unsatisfied by the new amp power Lizzie carry with them.

I realised then that I would have to write to you. My CV reveals that I can hold down a reporter's job (even allowing for the little exaggerations we all succumb to), but it doesn't tell you how much I know about rock. I would like to do that in person and if you have an editorial vacancy, no matter how humble, I would be grateful for the chance to tell you about myself.

Yours faithfully.

I thought that application showed a certain style and I met the writer. He joined the magazine I was running as assistant editor about six months after I received his letter. I was attracted to his oblique method of asking for a job and I found that the clippings he had attached to his CV contained a similar strain of weary humour. I always believed that writing style was the most important element in an application and it is necessary to demonstrate this as often as possible. The above letter is rather longer than I would have considered wise if I had been applying. Had it arrived on a day when I was putting the magazine to bed, or at some other hectic time, it might not have had the impact the writer hoped for. A year or so later I received the following plea.

December 1977

Dear Sir,

I am 24, fit, unmarried and healthy. I love heavy rock, but I also play jazz and odd things, such as Paul Simon and Billy Joel. I have interviewed several 'names' (cuttings enclosed) which I have sold as a freelance.

I am the youngest-ever sub on *The Evening Echo* and I loath it. I would, however, be delighted to undertake this role on your magazine if I also got the chance to interview artists and review records and concerts.

I look forward to hearing from you.

Yours faithfully,

This brief note was accompanied by several very impressive articles and the writer had no need to expound further in his letter. It was clear that he was not only a skilled journalist but was also knowledgeable about music, able to plan interviews well and had a good writing style. He also got a job.

The requirement for 'maturity' is one element that is subject to change. In the middle 1960s the writers on *NME* and *Melody Maker* were, in the main, very young and they often behaved irresponsibly. I those heady days, nothing mattered other than being young, being in music and writing about it.

By the middle seventies many of the same people were still in the music press, and just as the musicians had grown older so had the writers (many of whom had also grown quite tired). In the period between 1972 and 1978, the music business was in a good state financially and writers would often be taken on world tours at the expense of the record company or artists.

A complete change occurred in music when the punk movement started in 1975. It took a few years for this revolution to gain momentum, but by 1980 the business had undergone a complete transformation. Recession had completely altered the nature of the music business, as had the change in musical fashion, which occured when the 'boring old farts' (such as Alvin

53

Lee and Yes) were finally shouldered aside by newcomers.

The music press also convulsed. New editors and writers were needed who understood this 'horrible' new music. Inside a couple of years there was almost a complete change in the editorial staff of the big music papers. Only a few old-timers managed to hang on by changing their musical allegiance with chameleon-like speed. The change also resulted in a juxtaposition of the music papers and the emergence of several important new titles. When I joined *Sounds* in 1972 it was the avant-garde paper championing the new music (then Poco, CSN&Y, reggae, etc) but it has now been pushed into the role of the establishment paper, a position once occupied by *Melody Maker*. New, younger papers have sprung up to champion new music — *Smash Hits* being the most successful — and new writers have emerged to cover the music.

A major change also occurred in writing styles. I think the standard of writing in the music press is now higher than it has ever been and many of the journalists who held down jobs in the music press in previous decades wouldn't stand a chance now. To some papers, writing style is everything, and pop writers have to have a wide range of reference — looking into theatre, film and the fine arts as well as music.

Popular music is not in a very healthy state at the moment. Records are not selling well and to fill the number one spot in either the singles or album charts, a record has to sell only a quarter of the number necessary a decade ago. Pop music also lacks direction. Until 1980 there were always major trends in the business — soul, rock, pop, reggae, funk, supergroups, jazz rock, etc — and these would dominate the charts for shorter or longer periods. Today the charts are fragmented, much as they were before the arrival of rock'n'roll in 1956: middle-of-the-road acts will appear on *Top of the Pops* alongside ultra-new groups. At the moment, if the song is strong, if it is hyped well enough and if the accompanying video is attractive, the artist stands a chance no matter what style the song belongs to. That may sound healthy, but it does not create the sort of long lasting careers that developed songwriters such as Lennon and McCartney, Paul Simon, or Holland, Dozier, Holland.

For the above reason, you may be able to persuade an editor of a music publication that you have the right sort of knowledge to bring life to his journal. Editors are scared at the moment, they're scared of losing touch. Nobody knows what is coming next and the music scene is changing faster than ever before. Editors are terrified of being left behind, of seeming unfashionable and 'fashion' in its broadest sense must now be part of a music writer's armoury. At the moment, what the stars are wearing, what they're eating and where they're hanging out matters very much. This is almost a repeat of the 1960s attitudes, but at the moment fashion is even more ephemeral than the scribblings that followed Beatlemania. If you can convince an editor that you can write well and that you have your finger on the pulse, you stand a good chance. It doesn't matter where you live. It is not all happening in London. At the time of writing Liverpool is threatening to become ultra-fashionable again — this time in a very black and negative way (fashionable for being so appalling, really), but fashion is changing everywhere and your perception of that change is more important than your location.

You can best demonstrate your perception of fashion and music by writing about it. If you get nowhere with your application letters, send unsolicited articles to as many papers as you can. Don't photocopy the submission — editors resent simultaneous submissions — but if you can get access to a word processor you can produce articles that appear to be tailored for individual papers. Don't overdo the word-processor bit. If you send an article to a newspaper which is perfectly printed with justified left and right margins you will only attract suspicion and the editor will guess that all of his or her competitors received an identical article from you in that morning's post. Rejection will automatically follow. Print the article well, but do not justify the margins, do leave a couple of errors in the piece and use the cheapest paper. It works better.

If your articles are any good, and if you have been able to gauge what type of stories the paper is looking for, sooner or later one will be used and you will be paid. At that point you have the right to telephone the editor to ask about future possibilities. Don't scream at him for a job immediately, play it cool and ask about the possibility of future stories. Most editors are receptive to ideas from people who have proved they can produce publishable stories, and after you have succeeded in getting one or two stories in the paper, try to 'pop in' to the editorial office. You can use any pretext you like to cover your hustle, but do it nicely. Even if you live hundreds of miles away from the paper's office, it is still worth it to make a casual 20 minute visit. Tell the editor you have to visit a relation just round the corner and you would like to pop in to say hello. Meeting the editor is the greatest opportunity you can have. Editors, like most other people, prefer to employ people they like. It does happen that an editor will employ someone with a particular ability despite not liking them, but in the small, idiosyncratic world of a music publication, one's face usually has to fit.

When you visit the editor don't toady or try to be anything other than yourself. Don't put a suit or a 'smart'dress on, dress as you would when you go out for an evening (although avoid ultra extremes). The music press is an employment area that breaks all the rules careers advisors drum into you: editors are looking for people who belong to today, not to an older generation's vision of today. But your appearance must also indicate that you are not slavish to a particular fashion. If you were it would mean you couldn't change and you would, in time, become like the perpetual teds who lounge on street corner lampposts.

Don't take any of your work when you pop in to see the editor . . . if there's any suggestion that you're hustling you'll become the butt of jeering and jokes once you've left. Clutching an armful of cuttings or a scrapbook is very uncool. Unlike in America, in Britain it is acceptable to hustle only as long as you don't allow it to show. On rare occasions, gauche applicants can get away with arriving with a suitcase full of cuttings, a guitar or, as in one case I clearly remember, with their mother. In these rare circumstances only the most outstanding or charming personality will overcome the roars of hilarity from the young cynics who inhabit the world of the music paper. Chat about nothing, or about whatever the editor wants to talk about, and leave within half-an-hour. If you liked the editor it's a fair bet that he or she liked you and a note thanking them for their time and reminding them how keen you would be to apply for any vacancy that occurs is sufficient hustle. A week or two later send in another freelance story and keep waiting.

Whether you get your interview by repeated applications, or in a carefully orchestrated 'casual' situation such as the one above, you can do no more than show yourself. If one editor doesn't like you (or you don't like them), you can write that publication off until someone else takes over the chair.

If you get through the 'chat' you will probably get a job, if not immediately, then within a few months. Once in, you have to handle it properly.

Taking a 20-year-old (typically) from a quiet background, giving them the authority of an editorial position on a music publication and letting them loose is, I now realise, a very dangerous operation. A young person with an abiding love of music is suddenly given a key which unlocks all the doors to a world which had previously been closed. All of a sudden, perhaps within a couple of months, that young person will be attending record company receptions, chatting to stars, attending concerts and getting many free records. They might even get to travel on tour, although this type of coverage has waned since the recession struck.

The impressionable and enthusiastic often make the best writers, as they are able to communicate their fan-like enthusiasms to the thousands of fan readers who would give their right-arms to be allowed to visit a particular star in his or her dressing room. But the current style is for the music writers to play it cool, to put down the occasion or the event; this is merely an adolescent stance and it doesn't obscure the delight and wonderment that the writer feels and the fans want to read about.

Within a very short space of time, perhaps six months, the new music writer will have become cool (an outdated word, yet descriptive) or will have left the paper. It is not done to arrive at a small party held in honour of a big star and rush up and demand his autograph: music writers never do that. They are part of the business themselves and the most they are allowed is a 'hi' across the room. Behave like a fan and you won't be allowed to go. It's rather like making kids the owners of a sweetshop and telling them they mustn't eat sweets, but that is the way the game is played. Stars won't expose themselves to fan-like approaches from within the business and the hypocritical game must be played by the rules. (Stars of long-standing often yearn for more honesty in the proceedings and, on several occasions, I have suffered interviews that have gone badly wrong when a star has decided to break these unwritten rules.)

After another six months most music writers become cynics. Just as it is wearisome and far from glamorous for a star to give eight interviews a day, writers can become jaded by the experience of talking to three stars a day. It doesn't happen so much these days — there aren't that many stars around, but the principle applies. Meeting your first few big stars is always a thrill, but after that the pressures of deadline, your questions for the next interview and your concern about whether your expenses are going to be signed, take over. In short, the stars are taken out of your eyes. The business is revealed for what it is, a business, and your role is clearly defined. You, and your paper, are manipulated by the heavy money of the business (the record companies, the managers) and even if your publication rails against this and takes the stance of aggressor, you will still have to play by the rules which govern the big game — money making.

By the end of your first year you will have a much more realistic attitude to music journalism, and you must then decide whether it is a career you wish to pursue. Some writers opt to go into the business proper, becoming publicity agents, managers and even record producers. Others choose to remain in the no-man's land of the press and progress up the ladder of the music paper hierarchy, aiming eventually at the power which goes with the editor's chair. Having said all papers and writers are manipulated by the money, it is fair to say that editors of successful music papers wield considerable power, although they rarely realise the extent of it at the time they hold it.

One particular editor of a mass-selling weekly paper conducted a private experiment a few years ago. For reasons which will become obvious, I am not about to name him or the paper, but he decided to promote a type of music which had previously had little exposure in Britain. He picked it quite calculatingly and without having any financial interest in the success or failure of his experiment. He repeatedly ran front page stories and inside leads on the music and its exponents and within a few months he had built up a tidal wave within the business.

The other papers began to report on the music because they were afraid they were missing out on a new fashion. The radio and TV people began to think that they were also behind and rapidly rushed crews to where they could get interviews or footage, and record company people decided to try and sign the acts which the editor had featured most often.

It is important to point out that it was an academic experiment, he was not bribed, or induced to promote this music, I think he merely wanted to test his own power. (In fact I have *never* come across any direct bribery in the music press. There is certainly bribery in kind, about which more later, but I have never heard of a direct payment being made for journalistic favours.)

I think the editor was disillusioned after his experiment. Despite wielding this considerable power — and even lowly scribes have some measure of autonomous power — he had only been able to line the pockets of the record companies. Many of the music makers for whom he had a genuine feeling, remained as poor and as exploited as they had been previously. The kudos his paper got for 'discovering' the music got him an extra £500 a year, but he felt that he was used by everybody, despite the fact that it had been at his own instigation. Not long afterwards he moved to a record company (one that had benefitted greatly from the boom) and became a record producer. Now, ten years later he is completely out of the business.

The bribery in kind which is offered to writers usually takes the form of trips to interesting or exotic locations, free records and concert tickets, and for those writing about musical instruments, extended loans of various instruments and gadgets. The principle used to be a kind of unspoken blackmail, 'If you want any more trips like this one, you'd better write lots of nice things about our artists.'

I recall one trip which backfired in a big way, however. It was one of the most expensive and exotic trips I ever experienced in the music business. Uriah Heep produced an album called *High and Mighty* in 1976 and Gerry and Lillian Bron, their managers, hit on the ultimate promotion for the album. I received a call inviting me to lunch a few days later. I was told to be at my front door at 7a.m. with my passport but was told nothing else. A limousine collected this rather bemused and sleepy writer and I was driven to a small private airfield. A twin-engined light plane was taxi-ing for take off as my limo raced across the grass. I ran through the slipstream to grab the trailing hand that yanked me into the cockpit.

I found that the arm belonged to Gerry Bron and before I had a chance to ask where we were going we had taken off and were battling against a very bumpy headwind, crossing London at 1,500 ft to avoid the jet lanes. The trip was exhilarating, despite the early hour and, as we landed at Gatwick, I once again found myself running across tarmac in propeller slipstream. This time, the plane was a rather larger Dart Herald and I clambered on board at the very last moment to find an already hysterical guitarist (Mickie Box) opening bottles of champagne. The Herald had been converted into a flying bar and the twenty huge armchairs which had been bolted to the fitted carpet were occupied by some of the best-known TV, radio and press faces in the rock media. We were all given headphones — which supplied our first taste of what *High and Mighty* sounded like — and a constant supply of champagne, from very pretty stewardesses, ensured that we didn't notice the fact that no breakfast was served (there had been some catering hitch).

The stately progress of the old Herald and the hour's time difference conspired to land us in Berne about midday, well behind schedule. The Mayor of Berne and the brown bear (actually a man-filled skin) which is the symbol of that beautiful city, were on the small airfield to greet us and a brass band struck up an 'oom-pah-pah' of welcome. Uriah Heep and the press corps staggered down the mobile steps to find another champagne reception laid out on trestle tables on the tarmac; but, because we were behind schedule, we charmers of the music business only managed to take a glass of bubbly in each hand as we passed the tables and walked straight on to the bus which was waiting for us, just as the Mayor started his speech of welcome.

The bus whisked us away from the gesticulating mayor and the dancing bear and took us to the foot of the Schilthorn, a peak beside the Eiger. As might be expected, only one type of beverage was available during the hour's journey. This extended period of 'fortification' gave all of us enough Dutch courage to tumble out of the coach and gaze up at the longest cable car ride in the world without a twinge of nerves. More buses started arriving at the cable car station and I dimly realised that Bronze (UH's record label) had flown in writers and broadcasters from all over Europe.

We started the ascent in relays, the enthusiastic members of the band enjoying the joke of running from end to end of the cable car I was in to see how far they could make it swing on its axis. They then jumped up and down together to see how far the cable would sag. Despite the fact that many of us in the car had also enjoyed the hospitality during the flight, this activity

61

seemed a little unnecessary. (The horror on the cable car attendant's face also caused me some concern!)

A revolving restaurant is perched on the very top of the Schilthorn. It is a unique building, which was featured in the James Bond film *On Her Majesty's Secret Service*, known then, and since, as The Piz Gloria. The name lent itself to several appropriate jokes, especially as there was a Gloria in our party, and eventually we were all led out to the helicopter platform to admire the view and to enjoy (you've guessed it) another champagne reception. The restaurant is 11,000 ft (3,350 m) above sea level and it offers quite the most breathtaking view of the Alps I have ever seen. I hung onto the rail, above what seemed like a vertical drop, and even after my strenuous morning, I was temporarily sobered by the soaring majesty that was all around me.

We suffered the local welcome of Alpine horns, drank the champagne offered and trooped into the revolving restaurant. It was at this point that the incredibly expensive lunch party started to go wrong.

I estimated that there were several hundred journalists and broadcasters present and they had been flown in from Germany, Denmark, Holland, Scandinavia, France and several other European territories. There were also some of the best-known faces from British television present and as I sat down in a window seat I mentally totalled up what Bronze must have spent to provide all of them with the limousines, the connecting flights and the buses to assemble them all on top of a remote Swiss mountain for a *High and Mighty* lunch.

As the world slowly went by (and it did seem as if the world was below us) I began to feel less than well. At first I put it down to the alcohol intake, but as I struggled with the first course, I noticed that a long-serving, and very famous, Radio 1 DJ had gone face down in his soup. Suddenly everyone was complaining about feeling strange; and by the time I got to the lavatory the queue to be sick was unbelievable. We were all ill in (or out) of turn as our symptoms demanded (even the stars proving they were human), and suddenly someone realised the cause. We all had altitude sickness. Five hours previously we had been at ground zero, now we were perched on top of the world with alcohol dehydration. The scramble to the cable cars was, to say the least, undignified and on the journey down even Mickie Box and Ken Hensley were subdued. The moment we got to the bottom of the mountain most of us began to feel better, but not, I suspect, the organisers who had left behind the specially ordered (and painstakingly delivered) food and drink that sat virtually untouched 11,000 ft above us.

It was a quieter band of musicians and media people which made the return flight to Britain, as I should imagine it was on all the other chartered planes as they headed for different European destinations. A couple of the hardier members revived enough to open yet more champagne, but I was glad to get home.

That stunt cost a fortune. It got Uriah Heep a lot of column inches, and whether it paid for itself is something only Bronze will know. The band broke up shortly after and thus denied the company the chance to capitalise on its investments.

Lavish launches are now very rare in the music business. I described this event to show how excessive the whole thing can be, but it wouldn't be right to assume that the event assured the band of good record reviews. The reviews were 'mixed' but, not surprisingly, plenty of stories about the trip filled the papers and the airwaves the following week. That's bribery in kind.

After the punk revolution, many of the new generation of writers didn't hesitate to bite the hand that fed them and for a few months it was hilarious to spot the vitriolic attacks which often followed an expensive jaunt. Not surprisingly, the trips dried up.

The recession also took its toll, of course, and there is now less bribery in kind than there was ten years ago. The old 'glamour touch' is creeping back into the business and star-struck writers can be relied on to write mountains of gush if they are allowed to spend a day or two with their idols.

I mentioned earlier that writing for the music press is a short

Dave Cash — Capital Radio DJ, former programme controller of Bristol's Radio West (named after TV's Shoestring) and veteran of the pirate radio ships. 'The Kenny and Cash Show' on Radio London featured Dave Cash and Kenny Everett in 1966.

career. This is simply because most writers grow out of writing about pop music. The close association with the business does inhibit development, and by the time journalists are 35, few want to continue spending their evenings at ear-splitting gigs. If they don't move over willingly, the business can be relied on to change direction and leave them stranded.

'Is there life after *Sounds* . . . ?' used to be a popular question when I was on the paper, and the answer is definitely in the negative for some types who suffered from arrested development. Some writers get so caught up in the business that they become publicity agents, record producers, managers or even musicians. Only a few survive. Several well-known writers of the 1960s whose words entranced the millions who were then buying weekly pop papers are now dish-washing, drinking or unemployed.

The sort of place music journalists are 'allowed' to visit once they get a job on a music paper. This is the home Alvin Lee bought for himself in the early 1970s, and where he entertained visiting journalists.

A few 'grow up' and quit the business altogether. They change their hair style, apply for jobs as sub-editors on provincial papers, take on a mortgage and retire to gentle obscurity with a set of memories which will always separate them from their neighbours on the executive housing estates.

Only a handful can become editors in the music press (and I have illustrated the disillusionment of one editor above) and even fewer can progress to management or directorship within the publishing empire.

There is no practical way to start out on your own in music journalism. Locally produced gig-sheets and magazines are nearly always doomed to failure unless they are supported by an inappropriate amount of capital, and even when a music publication is launched on a national scale by an experienced publishing company, the odds are against it succeeding.

65

I believe that a writer on a major music paper gets very close to knowing what it is like to be a pop star without actually being one. Writers get the travel, a measure of personal success and a feel for the business which can't be got any other way. Only roadies and members of the band's personal management get closer to the life style. Being a music writer is an exciting but short career.

Radio is entirely different to music journalism, although the work pattern of the radio worker has similar patterns to the music business journalist. In discussing careers in radio, I make no excuse for excluding the job of DJ. The disc jockey is a performer in his or her own right and should be regarded as similar to a musician: just as this book is not a description of careers for musicians, neither is it a guide to working as a performer in radio.

Radio stations offer many exciting jobs which attract musically-orientated people who do not wish to perform. Producing music programmes must be the ultimate goal but, as in everything else, beginners have to start at the bottom.

Dave Cash, former programme director of Bristol's commercial radio station Radio West, and star presenter on Capital Radio explains what he looks for when employing a youngster.

> 'I look first for the right type of personality. Willingness is everything and some people have it and some people don't. I expect a school leaver to have some 'O level' qualifications, but examination passes aren't nearly as important as the right approach to work. On a radio station there may be official start and stop times, but it never works out that way in practice. You work until you are able to go home. There's no overtime pay and the person who worries about overtime payment isn't the right person for the job. You've got to love what you do.'

The sort of work available to a school leaver on a radio station is likely to be junior administrative work. It won't be like office work in a normal organisation as most of the tasks to be done concern programming or running the station. Juniors will be 'gofers' for technicians, DJs, producers and executives and will slowly find their own way into the station's workload. Most local radio stations have close contact with their public and this involves many community activities such as charity events, competitions and general assistance. The junior is likely to find him or herself sifting through thousands of competition entries, distributing second-hand toys or chasing record companies for certain records required for a programme.

The only way to get a job on a radio station is to write and ask for one. Vacancies for juniors don't occur often, but if you don't apply you certainly won't get one.

Dave Cash: 'I think all applications ought to be neatly laid out, explaining why the person wishes to work in radio. All the background details should be on a separate CV. If a letter is well presented, I usually try to see the person and if they've got a spark — I can only call it that — I'll remember them until the next job occurs. Then I'll probably interview them again.'

Dave has employed at least one young person through the Youth Opportunities Scheme and many local radio stations are acutely aware of the unemployment problems which surround them.

'Radio stations get hundreds of applicants,' explains Dave, 'but they're not necessarily looking for the best qualified person. A radio station is a very friendly place as well as a very busy place and the first requirement is that the person should fit in. They usually offer someone a trial first to make sure the applicant suits them and they suit the applicant.'

Once employed by a radio station in a dogsbody capacity, the successful junior (the one who has managed to join the station's permanent staff) has to choose the area he or she wishes to specialise in. The four main areas in a radio station are: programme making, advertising sales (in commercial stations),

Not all assignments for music journalists are glamorous. Here the author (right) suffers an explanation of the merits of an acoustic chamber during a visit to an Electro-Voice factory in Switzerland.

68

administration, technical services and news. The news and technical services departments usually demand qualified entrants and don't have much to do with the music business, but the other departments regularly take on juniors without vocational qualifications.

If you want to work in music radio and you get a chance to enter a station in any department, take the chance. If you prove you can 'fit in' then it isn't difficult to move within the station. If you prove to be good at selling advertising airtime you can make a lot of money in radio (see the selling section in the chapter on musical wholesaling for an idea of what this entails), but most other departments offer a great deal of job satisfaction but only average wages.

BBC local radio stations are more difficult to get into. On the other hand, they provide entry to 'Auntie BBC', a unique institution which is, quite rightly, the envy of the broadcasting world. The old joke is that you need a degree even to clean the lavatories at the BBC and, sadly, there is some truth in it. The BBC are extremely snobbish about their intake and I suppose they can afford to be. Like most large organisations, the BBC is riddled with bureaucratic nonsenses and, as a result, the red tape regulations often leave the person with the 'right' personality out in the cold while simultaneously placing an academic square peg in a round hole. BBC departments all over the country are filled with such square pegs who are shunted sideways until they no longer grate on anyone's nerves. And their sinecures are paid for by our licence money. Having made that criticism, I must point out that the right person, having gained entry, has the broadcasting world at his or her feet. The BBC training is second to none in scope and quality and if your ambition is to be a Radio 1 producer or a *Top of the Pops* camera man, all things are possible once inside the organisation.

The BBC is the exception to the 'write and write again' rule. If you don't have the right qualifications — usually a degree — you can't get in. It doesn't seem to matter what type of degree you have (unless you're going for a high-powered job). One

69

friend of mine offered her degree in Russian and was put into the picture library, another offered an American degree from a Seattle university which he cheerfully insisted was inferior to the British '11 plus' and he's now the producer of a Radio 4 arts programme. If you've got a degree and want to work in music radio, you'll probably get into the BBC if you are prepared to travel and work in small town radio and if you apply often enough.

Radio has exploded in the last ten years. New commercial radio stations are continuing to open up every few months and the White Paper on the future of BBC radio in the 1990s points to further development of the local network. This means that for school or college leavers dedicated to finding a job in radio, the prospect, although not an easy one, is better than ever before.

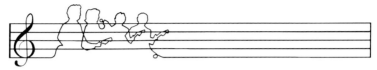

4
WORKING IN
MUSICAL INSTRUMENT
RETAILING

Without going on the road, it is impossible to get closer to the
world of the musician than working in a musical instrument
shop. To outsiders, these often grubby little shops, tucked away
in the back streets of the cities appear unprepossessing, if not
downright sordid, but for the local musical community a good
music store is the equivalent of a social centre.

Musical instrument shops sell amplification equipment and
accessories as well as musical instruments and if you have no
interest in the mechanics of making music, then the idea of
working in such an environment will hold little attraction for
you. At one time record shops provided interesting employment
for young people who loved records (without, necessarily,
loving music making) but today many record outlets are self-
service and the few specialist shops which do exist have very few
vacancies to offer the thousands of would-be employees.

You won't get a job in a music shop without knowing something about musical instruments, but you don't have to be a
great musician, or even a competent one. The last thing any
music shop wants is a player who's going to sit in the store and
play flashy runs which will drive customers away in embarrass-
ment, but you do have to play sufficiently well to demonstrate
an instrument for a shy or non-playing customer.

Most music shops are dirty, sleazy places, but not all! This is Graham Pell's 'Music Futurestore' in Leicester and it is one of the few music shops in Britain that manages to look attractive and sell musical instruments at the same time.

There are just over 1,000 musical instrument shops in Britain (excluding electronic organ stores) and although the recession

has forced some to close, new ones always seem to open in their place. At one time, music shops invariably seemed to be run by members of the older generation who were often hopelessly out of touch with modern music. Although there are still a few such shops about (you can spot them by their faded amber Celluloid sun shields) most are now owned by younger ex-musicians who

73

Some of the largest
music shops have
separate departments.
The staff shown here
work at the Rose-
Morris showroom in
London's Shaftesbury
Avenue.

have decided that there is more money to be made from selling instruments than by playing them.

Music shops which sell group instruments are traditionally filthy places. I remember calling into a well-known music shop in Demark Street, London's Tin Pan Alley, a few years ago. The carpet in the shop may, at one time, have had a colour, but the years of wet and greasy footfalls had encrusted it with a material which had formed a shiny black surface. On this occasion I got through the door and stumbled over a world-famous guitar hero who was on his hands and knees gently licking the revolting 'lino'. I gathered that he had accidentally dropped an illegal substance and was loath to do without it. Rock musicians are used to shopping in dirt.

There have been several gallant attempts to offer musicians better shopping facilities. One of the first 'super' music stores was opened in London's Tottenham Court Road in 1975. This was the first Fender Soundhouse and this superbly lit and equipped store offered musicians a chance to sit down on luxurious couches, take coffee at a well-equipped coffee bar and study instruments whilst standing on new shag-pile carpet. Tragically, this spot-lit emporium burnt down before any real assessment could be made of its appeal to musicians, but later experiments have suggested that this type of shop is not to the taste of rock musicians.

Quite why musicians like untidy and dirty shops is not clear. It is certainly true that British musicians — unlike their American cousins — find it desperately hard to make a living unless they are lucky enough to have a hit record, and it may be the resultant poverty ethic which makes them suspicious of the profit margins which have to be made to support a swish shop. A few stores — Kitchens of Leeds, Nottingham's Carlsbro Sound Centre and Liverpool's Hessey's for example — have successfully broken the mould, but most retail outlets seem to have remained unchanged for 25 years.

A music shop is not the place for those who are fastidious about working conditions. The loo is likely to be appalling and there is never enough room for stock. The nearest thing to a staff room is likely to be an attic filled with cartons and I get the strong feeling that both musicians and music shop workers choose not to have it any other way.

Despite this embedded conservatism, there is a powerful wind of change blowing through musical instrument retailing. The change is being caused by the computer — not in its role of stock keeper or accounts manager, but in its role as musical instrument. The computer is, of course, changing almost everything else in life, but its effect on music (as I have explained in my book, *The Musician and the Micro* also published by Blandford Press), is nothing short of revolutionary. Music shop owners and assistants have two choices — learn about computers, or watch their customers go elsewhere.

The companies which distribute computer-based instruments, Roland UK for example, realise that the computer has brought a whole new discipline to an area where, previously, the principal need had been for knowledge of guitar necks and drum shells. The new generation of musicians want to use micro-based instruments to make music more easily and they will choose the shop which offers them the widest range and the best service. Roland is now frantically training retailers to understand the new technology, but it is inevitable that some older retailers will reject the change and will, ultimately, pay the price. If you understand the principles of computers, and you play a musical instrument, you may be well-qualified to find a job in a music store. (There is more about the necessary skills later in this chapter.)

If you work in a music shop you are bound to meet a star sooner or later. Many music shops have their own clutch of local stars whom they look after well and touring stars often drop into provincial shops to talk about a repair problem or consider a new instrument. Contrary to popular opinion, very few stars are supplied with free instruments by the manufacturers and most are only too pleased to have earned enough money to be able to buy the instruments of their choice.

Star musicians consider a music shop to be a 'safe' place where they won't be molested by fans. They expect, and usually get, fawning service, but they don't expect to sign autographs and answer questions about their latest album. They may choose to discuss such subjects, but that must be left to them, otherwise the stars will rapidly decide that they can't relax enough to consider their purchases properly and will go elsewhere.

The making of a purchase, or the consideration of a purchase, is the only pretext many music shop owners will accept for a musician's presence in a shop. Many musicians are out of work and the store owner who allows musicians to 'hang out' may benefit from personal popularity, but he or she is likely to suffer from a crowded shop and irritated *bona fide* purchasers. Despite this, the owner and assistants must befriend all local musicians, yet find a way to kick unemployed musicians out whilst, at the same time, making them feel they're always welcome. It's not easy, but good dealers are masters at the art.

If you decide to try and find employment in a music store, you can't expect to start on a good wage. Some of the smaller music shops pay 'cash in hand' and choose to break the law by not paying national insurance contributions on your behalf. In these circumstances it is often tacitly understood that you are responsible for paying, or not paying, your own income tax, but the employer is still breaking the law by making this arrangement. You might consider putting up with this type of situation if the job is very temporary — a few weeks for example — but the system will work against you if you accept it for a longer period.

Although it is true that you may receive less in your hand at the end of the week when you are properly employed, the benefits you receive by having tax deducted at source and your stamp paid for you outweigh the extra £10 in your pocket. A spell on the dole is now likely for all adult workers in Britain and every worker must understand that not paying insurance stamps and joining the so-called black economy is not only robbing fellow unemployed workers of their unemployment benefit, but will also directly affect their own ability to draw dole money when the time comes. It isn't worth it. If you were to be foolish enough to put up with this situation for a sustained period, you would also be throwing away your right to protection under the Employment Protection Act.

Some shops offer assistants commission on sales, most do not. If you are a good salesperson you will quickly find your wages increasing. Music shop owners work on the premise that every new assistant is likely to be dishonest, unsuitable or unwilling. It's sad, but true. For that reason you must expect to start off on a tiny wage surrounded by the expectation that you won't stay very long. Perhaps it is because the wages are so appalling, perhaps it is because of the temptation which exists in every shop job, but many assistants steal from their employers. Unlike some of the bigger stores, music shops make no allowance for staff pilfering and if you steal items from the shop you will either 'get sorted out', taken to court or just tossed out. (I saw a delightful sign in a small Scottish musical instrument shop once. The owner was a huge bruiser with a broken nose, probably an ex-bouncer or roadie. The sign read, 'Shoplifters will be discouraged by the management.')

You don't need any formal qualifications to work in a music shop, but you need to know something about instruments and you must have a pleasant personality. You must also be honest and you must be capable of the simple mental arithmetic of change giving.

The preserve of the music shop is, sadly, almost exclusively male (most of the music business remains in the Dark Ages when it comes to equality of opportunity), but I have met two very successful female music shop assistants. The argument against inviting females into the business runs along the lines of 'It's one place where the boys swap stories and like to feel uninhibited.' It's plain those unfortunate boys don't know the girls very well, they have far better stories!

The only way to get a job in a musical instrument shop is to go in and ask. Do make sure that you've got hold of the owner or manager, there's no point in talking to an assistant. Tell him or her (there are a few lady owners, by the way — Ann Mellor of A1 Music, Manchester springs to mind) that you would like to work in a musical instrument shop and tell them why you think you would be suitable. Tell them which instrument you play and tell them that you read the musicians' magazines. It's unlikely that there will be a vacancy just at the moment you pop in, so ask if you can leave your name and address with the owner. Write it out neatly on a piece of paper and hand it over. You will, of course, be unlikely to hear anything. Call in a month or so later and don't get discouraged if you never seem to catch the owner. Keep calling in, but avoid Saturdays if you can — no one is likely to have time to chat to you. Remind the owner who you are and what you want and if a job comes up you will stand a fair chance of getting a phone call or a post card. It's worth handing out new slips of paper each time you visit as your first offering is almost certain to be discarded.

If you are eventually offered a job in a music shop, don't haggle about the wages that are suggested. If the owner wants to pay you in cash and dodge the law, try and change his or her mind, and if you feel that your request might endanger your chance of getting the job, ask if you can be transferred to the official payroll if you prove yourself reliable after a couple of months. Most will agree to this and you will have to keep working on the ones who won't.

After getting the job, you have to try and make yourself indispensable to the manager or owner — that is the only way of winning an increased salary. The way to do this is to sell instruments. This doesn't mean that you've got to force instruments down customer's throats — the music shop is no place for the hard sell — but you've got to pursue a sale. When you've handed over the drum sticks asked for, it's always worth asking if the customer needs any new drum heads, shell cleaner or similar accessories. In a music shop it is more a question of seeing opportunities than going into a 'hard sell'. The best assistants are always chirpy, appear to chat nonchalantly with

The type of instrument to be found in a music shop is changing rapidly. This display of musical computers and analogue synthesizers is typical of the sort of equipment that the successful sales assistant will have to understand.

customers whilst making sure the correct change is given and they always remember to enquire if there is anything else the musician needs.

Use the spare time which always crops up in shop-work to get thoroughly knowledgeable about all the different instruments. If the shop sells second-hand gear — and most do — sort out the wheat from the chaff (if necessary, by picking someone else's brains) and choose your customers carefully before letting them know there's a special bargain 'just come in'. You will rapidly

81

learn about a wide variety of instruments in addition to the instrument you play and it is only through understanding the needs of a drummer (for example) that you can discuss with him the merits of a new bass drum pedal which won't break during heavy stage use.

New instruments offer good salespeople wonderful opportunities. Get to grips with new synthesizers which come in, and if you can understand them before the boss, you are well on the way to making yourself invaluable to the store. If you understand microcomputers, you may well find this knowledge to be a real lever. Computer instruments are getting cheaper and cheaper to buy and you can best keep up with the technology by reading the specialist musicians' magazines and the computer publications. Showing a brand new instrument to an affluent regular customer as though he or she is getting a 'first' look at it is a great sales aid. Even if you cannot make a sale on the spot, you may well plant the germ of a future sale.

As an assistant, you will naturally have to put up with all of the tedious chores such as message running and sandwich buying. If you take this on with a smile, whilst concentrating on building your sales ability, you will soon be considered too valuable an asset to waste in this way and these duties will be shoved on to somebody else.

There are always difficult jobs in a music shop at which you might choose to become proficient, thus earning yourself a respected place. Hire-purchase is one area which is always difficult when musicians are involved. It is hard to think of a less suitable candidate for hire-purchase than a musician. Usually young, broke and footloose, most credit companies would rather run a mile than give them credit, but despite this, thousands of HP applications submitted by musicians are accepted each week.

In order to ensure the successful completion of a sale it is often advisable for an assistant or manager in the music shop to go through the HP form with the hopeful musician. The replies to the questions must, of course, be accurate but, like all form filling, there are better and worse ways to put things. If you become adept at handling these forms, you will certainly be able to carve a niche for yourself. If you develop useful contacts inside the HP company, you will become even more valuable to the store. Despite the outward appearances of credit companies, decisions about whether or not to grant credit in border-line cases often hang on the whim, or rather the instinct of a particular credit manager. One or two of the most successful music shop owners I know owe much of their success to their ability to persuade credit managers that their customers are good risk. It is not wise to suggest that a bad risk is a good one — that will only devalue your opinion in the future — but in border-line cases the shop may have known the customer for several years and can offer the credit company an unofficial character reference. This type of assistance is always informal, but can prove invaluable.

You may choose to specialise in one of the shop's departments. A large music shop may have many different departments, sometimes on different floors and if your particular interest is in guitars, computer instruments, drums or brass, you may be able to develop specialised knowledge which will prove of value both to you and the shop. The larger shops often have classical departments and if you have a particular interest in classical music, you may find yourself in charge of sheet music or classical instrument sales.

When a band is considering the purchase of a large item, such as a PA system or mixing desk, some shops are prepared to take the system out to a concert to allow the band to try it out under 'live' conditions. You may enjoy this part of the work and you may develop a speciality such as sound mixing.

This leads us into an important subsidiary area of the musical instrument trade — hire. Equipment hire was virtually unknown in the 1960s, but as the costs of musical equipment escalated, particularly the cost of PA systems, it became an economic feasibility for shops to hire out systems on a nightly or weekly basis. Many specialised hire companies sprang up, and many shops developed separate departments to handle the work. If you are interested in PA systems or sound mixing you may gravitate to one of these departments or to a hire company. There are some hire companies which rent out conventional musical instruments, but most hire companies only offer PA items and the more expensive, exotic equipment such as dedicated computer musical instruments.

If you are a success at musical instrument retailing, the natural progression is to open your own music shop. There are still openings for experienced managers, but you will never gain quite the satisfaction (or remuneration) you will if you run your own shop.

Although, on the face of it, it needs a considerable amount of capital to rent a shop, fit it and fill it with stock, the musical instrument business is so small that people who have spent more than a couple of years in the industry become well known. This becomes an advantage when an established and successful sales assistant decides to set up shop on his or her own. Wholesalers are prepared to grant credit to a retailer who has a proven track record and is known personally. This doesn't remove the need for capital, but it does considerably reduce the amount required.

Other 'promotion' avenues (from music shops) lead to road management, musical instrument wholesaling and, in many instances, into bands.

If you have a love, or special feeling, for musical instruments, working in a music shop can be a very pleasant way of earning a living.

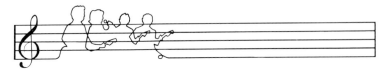

5
WORKING IN MUSICAL INSTRUMENT WHOLESALE

If you like music *and* people, and you know something about musical instruments, you might well be suited to a job in the wholesale musical instrument industry.

Although it is a small industry compared with some — TV or hi-fi for example — this is one of the delights of the 'MI' trade (as it is called). Everybody gets to know everybody else, which makes it a fun industry to work in and offers the chance to make good and lasting friendships.

There are drawbacks in working in a small industry, however, and if you're lazy, dishonest or just incompetent you can be sure that your reputation will always precede you.

Musical instrument wholesalers fall into two broad categories: those which make and distribute musical instruments, and those which simply distribute instruments made by others. It is only in recent years that companies have begun to distribute their own products, but a competitive market has led more and more companies to consider this move and today there are a variety of trading patterns in the market-place.

Some companies import and export musical merchandise, distribute thousands of items — from piccolos to guitar strings. Such companies may be fairly described as 'wholesale jobbers'. Other companies, especially the newer electronics-based

More and more musical equipment companies are 'cutting out the middle-man' and selling their own products directly to the musician. Here, Custom Sound mixers are assembled in Britain's West Country before direct distribution to the purchasers.

companies, import or make one or two lines of musical merchandise and concentrate on making these successful. This type of small operation has proved very efficient in the last few years and the larger, general purpose, distributors of musical products have all trimmed their sails in order to compete. It seems that the era of the wholesaler with thousands of stock items is coming to a close.

For a person who likes travelling, the ultimate aim — of

becoming an international salesperson in musical instruments — is one worth considering. There are traditional manufacturers and wholesalers who deal exclusively in the 'non pop' area of music; band instruments, orchestral instruments and school merchandise. There are many wholesalers who choose to operate in this traditional field, and although some of them have flirted with the idea of supplying instruments and other equipment intended for use in popular music, they usually stick to the markets they know best — military bands, marching bands, schools, orchestras and similar organisations.

Before dismissing the idea of working in such a 'dull' area, consider the fact that such wholesalers sell their products all over the world. The successful overseas salesperson can earn a fortune and can spend half of his or her life travelling to exotic parts of the world, taking orders to equip the Borneo military band (for example) or kitting out a new school of music in Mexico. In addition, many British and American companies sell their 'rock' instruments and amplification equipment on the 'world' market. Very few manufacturers now consider individual territories, most look for every chance to export and the international salesperson has become one of the most important figures in all manufacturing industries.

You don't get to be an international salesperson just by asking, of course. The requirements include a thorough knowledge of the products, a thorough knowledge of the potential markets for the instruments and, on top of all this, an ability to sell and to follow through and ensure the order is delivered satisfactorily (and paid for!). Skill with foreign languages is, of course, a considerable advantage.

If you are serious about considering a career in the more traditional side of music wholesaling, you will need to provide yourself with a particular skill which will appeal to one of the more successful distributing companies.

One skill you may already have is the ability to play a musical instrument. The value of that skill depends on how well you can play it and on which instrument you play. Although salespeople

87

Wholesaling imported goods demands that all necessary supplies of spares are carried. Here American-made Crate amplifiers await distribution while shelves bulge with unassembled circuit boards.

aren't often expected to give demonstration performances, a musical instrument salesperson will frequently be talking to musicians, and a thorough understanding of music is a great boon (although it is true to say that many very successful salespeople almost pride themselves on their inability to play a musical instrument).

The ability to play a few chords on a guitar is not likely to stand you in particularly good stead in an interview with the marketing manager of a musical instrument wholesale company. If you play a less common instrument, or if you really understand your instrument (especially its technology) then you will stand a better chance. A person who is thoroughly familiar with the various types of drum, the methods of manufacture, the variety of materials used and the problems which occur during the life of a set of drums, is going to be of far more use to a wholesaler than someone with the ability to play some fancy drum fills. Musical wholesalers have no place for frustrated and failed musicians. You may have considered playing music professionally at one period, but when you ask for an interview with a musical instrument wholesaler, you must be sure that you want to work with instruments for themselves, not because you hope they might provide a bridge back into playing.

Having said that, there are many 'failed' musicians in the musical instrument business. Many don't fail — they simply face up to reality, to getting married, to keeping a family and paying the rent or mortgage. For many it represents a mature choice. Entering the musical instrument industry allows ex-musicians to keep in touch with music, to work with and to meet other

Unfortunately trade shows are a necessary evil of musical instrument wholesaling. This shot, taken a few years ago at the world's largest musical instrument trade fair in Frankfurt, sums up the boredom of the event.

musicians and to earn a regular wage while still being close to their first love. There is nothing wrong with loving music and music-making, but it is vital that you have made a firm commitment to enter the *business* side of music before you go for an interview, otherwise you are wasting your time and the company's.

If you are lucky enough to be taken on by a musical instrument company while you are young, you are likely to be tried out in various departments to see what you do best. Every company is hoping that a super salesperson is going to walk through the door and at some stage you should expect to be pointed to a telephone and handed a list of musical instrument dealer addresses. The company will want to see if you are any good at selling on the telephone.

You will be expected to telephone each dealer in turn, introduce yourself and ask if there are any items the shop needs. Telephone selling can be a soul-destroying business but for people who prove themselves good at it, the rewards can be very high indeed.

Selling by phone has become very fashionable. It is, of course, far easier to sell something when you meet someone face to face, but the costs of sending salespeople out to meet potential customers are so high that many companies prefer to accept a lower success rate as a trade off against the high costs of travelling sales representatives. There is always another person to telephone, but the costs of visiting a customer unsuccessfully are the same whether or not a sale is made.

There are two main types of telephone selling. The first is 'repeat sales' when a salesperson rings an existing customer to enquire politely whether the company has anything the customer may need. This is the easier form of telephone selling. The second form is called 'the cold sell'. In this approach, the salesperson telephones someone who is not a customer and may not even have heard of the company the salesperson is representing. The most common forms of this second type of selling intrude into our daily lives, offering such products as double glazing, insurance and damp proofing.

'Hello, is that Swinford 773?'

'Yes . . .'

'Oh, good evening, sorry to disturb you . . . my name is Thompson . . . I'm from United Standard.'

'Yes . . .'

'I was wondering if we could meet, I think I may be able to help you with your savings . . .'

Usually the insurance salesperson hears the line go dead soon after this opening gambit. If he or she is a sensitive soul, a few such reactions will produce tedium, resentment and, finally, disillusionment. But for the resilient, ever-confident type who is prepared to go on listening to the dialling tone until the cows come home, the rewards can be considerable. Each attempted sale costs only a phone call and an eventual breakthrough will earn back far more than all of the costs incurred.

Thankfully, the musical instrument industry rarely resorts to the cold sell. As I mentioned before, the industry is very small, perhaps just over a 1,000 musical instrument retailers in the UK, and there isn't really room for such a sales method. But if you get into a sales department you should expect to be treated like a newcomer and, human nature being what it is, you can expect to get the unpleasant jobs to do. You may be handed a list of dealers who are not customers of the company and you may have to try to persuade them to become so.

There is a clearly defined ratio of success in telephone selling and the department's sales manager will know very well what this is. If you do get the chance to try your hand on the phone, and if you're unlucky enough to get a 'cold' list, content yourself with the knowledge that you are only expected to get one 'yes' decision in 20 *decisions*. Remember that word *decisions*. When you telephone a music shop you may get an engaged signal, you may get no answer (yes, even during the day!), you may get an answer but it may be that the manager or owner is not available. Only when you speak to the person who is able to say 'yes' or 'no' can you consider that you have received a decision. This means that you may have to make 60 phone calls to get 20 decisions. When you get your decisions, you can't rely on the '1 in 20' rule always working. Some days you will get three successes in 20, then you might go three days without a single success. The 1 in 20 is an average figure which is known throughout the sales industry.

A well-managed telephone sales department will expect every telephone salesperson to elicit no less than 35 definite decisions per seven hour working day. If the sales manager expects more, or if he or she demands a higher percentage of positive responses, they may either be behaving bloodily, they may not understand telephone selling or they may have hit on a new sales method about which the rest of the world knows nothing.

All sales departments provide new recruits with a 'spiel' to tell customers, but it is only when a phone call begins to turn positive that the salesperson has to think quickly and ensure that he or she can answer correctly the questions about price and availability of items. When a sale is agreed between two people, the salesperson is said to have 'closed' the sale, that is they have persuaded the customer to agree unequivocally to purchase something from them. The word 'unequivocally' is important. Any prevarication from the customer — 'well I think it might be OK for you to send the guitar straps' — will only mean problems later on. The goods may be returned. The customer may not pay for them. Certainly you will have lost your commission on the sales and regular occurrences of such 'misunderstandings' will ensure you leave the sales department fairly promptly. The customer must be forced to say that he or she definitely wants the guitar straps.

Most human beings abide by their word, *when that word is clearly given*, and when it is confirmed (by you) by a confirmation copy of the order being dispatched. If you follow this procedure, 99 times out of 100 the order will always go through. A telephone salesperson (or any salesperson for that matter) must ask clearly for the order — 'so may I send you 30 guitar straps?' — must wait in silence for the reply (the silence is very important), and when the confirmation comes, must repeat it so that no doubt exists in the customer's mind. Selling is a highly skilled occupation and it is my view that 70 per cent of people who describe themselves as salespersons haven't got the faintest clue about it. They get by just because they're nice; people do go out of their way to give their orders to nice people. Some sales people survive because they're paid very little and deliver the lowest possible percentage of success, the percentage that would fall into their lap just by making a phone call, and some survive through the inefficiency or indifference of their employers. But this high percentage of 'order takers' (as successful salespeople regard them) only serves to highlight the abilities of a clear minded salesperson.

There are two reasons why you may be given 'cold selling' when you first join the sales department of a musical instrument company. The first is that well-established companies may be loath to allow you free rein to insult their highly-valued customers, the second is the reason mentioned earlier: newcomers always get the dirty jobs. The joke turns sour on the established staff when the newcomer turns cold prospects into firm customers. If you do manage to get new customers for a company you can be sure you are making a good impression. No matter how small an order from a new customer, it is likely that in time the customer will become used to ordering from your company and the orders will grow. That is how every business is built up.

If you are allowed to telephone existing customers you will often get involved with details which will slow you down. You'll hear complaints about previous shipments. You'll have to find out why orders haven't been delivered and, in the early days, you'll be expected to know about things and people who are completely new to you. Always own up when you don't understand something. This is a good general rule in life, but it is especially important in selling. Every time you allow a reference to pass unexplained, you are digging a deeper hole for yourself in the future. Own up that you're new, own up to your inexperience and you'll nearly always get a helping hand.

Salespeople in musical instrument companies are usually paid a lowish basic wage which is designed to be topped up by a commission on sales. It almost goes without saying that if you don't make any sales you are stuck with the low basic wage, but you should always be able to sell something. Most commission structures allow even moderately successful salespeople to earn relatively high wages and if money is top of your list of job specifications, then you should give serious consideration to the idea of entering sales. Selling to existing customers nearly always produces less commission than bringing new customers to the company, and if you prove to be good at the cold sell, you can earn a fortune. The classified advertisements in the newspaper that say 'I'll show you how you can earn £50,000 a year like me' aren't kidding. It is just that the person who can succeed in cold selling is a rare and valuable animal. I think the qualities required are peculiarly un-British and this may be one more factor in Britain's trading decline.

The travelling sales representative in musical instruments is, sadly, a dying species. There are still some good ones travelling the highways and byways of Great Britain taking orders from dusty back street music shops, but better communications have signalled an end to this idiosyncratic breed. Until recent years, the annual London Hilton dinner held for its members by the Association of Musical Instrument Industries featured, as one of its more important events, a toast to 'the gentlemen of the road, past and present.' The dinner is now defunct, the Association has changed its name to eliminate the word Instrument and there are precious few 'gentlemen of the road' any more. Times are changing.

You cannot become a traveller (to use the pre-war term) in musical instruments without experience. It is possible that you could have gained experience as a sales representative in another industry (there are several still making good use of the travelling sales rep; food, fashion and bookselling, for example) or you may have worked your way up from the ranks of the telephone sales department, but you need to be mature and responsible before any company is prepared to provide you with an Escort or Sierra, a bag of samples and a tankful of petrol. It is all too easy for inexperienced reps to skive, but they don't last long if they do, and for many it's a short but merry life. The good ones are industrious and work long hours. They're away from home for weeks on end and they are meticulous in the worst chore of the job — paper work. You may be good at chatting to old Joe in the pub, but if you don't write down every order you've agreed with him (usually in triplicate) and dispatch it that night to your company, you're wasting your time. Reps take a lot of stick. When they walk into a shop they often walk into trouble. Some dealers think they can use the poor old rep as a whipping boy and if they've had a difficult customer, they take it out on the one person who can't be rude to them: a supplier's representative. A good rep will know his or her customers and will know how to handle them, but the gift for diplomacy and knowing when to beat a retreat is second only to the determination to win despite the difficulties the customer presents. These two qualities are in conflict and plague every salesperson.

If you are not attracted to a sales career (or if it is not attracted to you) there are several other departments in musical instrument wholesalers that may appeal.

The warehousing and dispatch of musical instruments demands a respect for the products, as many are extremely fragile. More and more instruments are using complex electronic circuitry and the packing for such instruments demands great care and attention.

If you are offered a job in warehousing or dispatch it means two things; the company expects that you are capable of ensuring that fragile and expensive items are transported without suffering damage and, more importantly, that the company is offering a position of trust to you. There is an element of security in every warehouse and you shouldn't be offended if there is an occasional spot check on clothes and lockers. It's not you the company is checking so much as its own system.

The clerical and accounts departments of musical instrument companies are similar to those of any other organisation involved in distribution and the employee in these departments is likely to have only second-hand contact with anything musical.

Promotion and advertising, however, are very different. Most musical instrument companies have a person responsible for the promotion and advertising of its products and some companies support sizeable promotion departments. In the past these have included photographic studios and print facilities, but as the recession has deepened most companies have pared down their staff to the minimum, preferring to 'buy in' such specialist services when required.

Strictly speaking, advertising and promotion are two separate areas of the overall sales philosophy of a company. This overall philosophy is called marketing. Advertising means the preparation of advertisements, the purchasing of space or air time and the insertion of the advertisements in the press and the other media. In addition, it usually includes 'below the line' activities such as preparing posters and cards for in-store display.

Promotion, on the other hand, has a far wider brief. Many American instrument companies hire promotion people just to hang out with the stars in the hope of persuading them to try, endorse or simply play one of that company's instruments. If it sounds a pretty idyllic job, you still haven't realised that the music industry is a *business*. The promotions people who hang about backstage and thrust unwanted guitars towards a star are often regarded as pimps, and the little job satisfaction they achieve (perhaps getting on to first-name terms with the star) is more than offset by the frustrations and torments they suffer at the hands of the star's entourage — the roadies, the tour managers and the press agents.

In Britain we are more genteel in our promotion, but that does not necessarily mean we are less effective. British instrument wholesalers *do* ask stars to play their instruments, but the approach is usually made more formally and the promotions person may be invited to a record session or an office to show the instrument in question.

Promotion may mean promotion of the product to either 'the trade' (dealers, distributors and the press) or 'the public' (meaning musicians). The first type of promotion may include such events as press receptions, in-store promotions and trade exhibitions. The second type of promotion may call for the arranging of demonstration concerts, the organisation of musical workshops and the mounting of displays at exhibitions for the public.

If you have had no experience in advertising or promotions, you can only hope to be taken on as the humblest of assistants. This is a very popular type of job, as certain aspects have similarities to journalism and the job involves considerable contact with the media. As any careers advisor will tell you, media jobs are perhaps the most sought-after jobs of all, both by school and college leavers. A position in a promotions department can lead to later entry to the media (usually by getting to know somebody already in the media), but because there are so many applications for jobs which even vaguely smack of publicity or public relations, employers are able to be very choosy.

The best skill you can offer an employer who is seeking someone for the advertising and promotion department is a high standard of English. This does not mean that you need to be an expert in the works of Shakespeare or Trollope. It means that you must be able to express yourself clearly and grammatically in both spoken and written English. Another skill that many promotion departments look for is artistic flair, particularly an understanding of graphic arts. Many promotion departments prepare their own advertisements and a basic artistic ability in this field will stand you in good stead. A secondary skill that is now proving useful is the ability to type. As cut-backs reduce secretarial staff and word-processors arrive, junior employees, male or female, with the ability to type accurately, prove much more self-sufficient within a company than the 'corridor creepers' who plead with a reluctant member of the typing pool to get a scruffy letter produced. If you are male and you consider typing to be a female activity, think again! The arrival of computers into almost every walk of life demands that we all type. The day of the female typist is nearly over.

With good English or art, perhaps some typing and a knowledge or understanding of musical instruments, you stand a fair chance of winning an opening in the advertising and promotion department of a musical equipment wholesaler. The duties are likely to be pleasant. The busiest time of year in a promotion department is around the time of the trade exhibitions — usually in the Spring and Autumn. This is the time when all of the dealers and overseas buyers visit trade exhibitions to plan their purchases for the coming year. The promotion department is likely to be kept very busy getting ready the designs and display material for the exhibition stand.

As in all sections of the media, advertising and promotion is not a career which tolerates clock-watchers. When you are busy you stay until the job is finished. If you have social arrangements you cancel them if the job demands it. Theoretically, employers allow staff to take time off when the department is less busy, but although the mainstream media follows this course, employers such as musical instrument companies tend to be traditional and are wary of offering the freedom of individual working hours to members of the promotion department. As stated, the compensation for all this is that your duties in the department are likely to be pleasant.

As an assistant you are unlikely to be allowed to buy advertising or create advertisements yourself. You may often be in the position of executing other people's ideas and this involves such tasks as getting instruments round to photographers, overseeing photographic sessions (this often means making sure the instruments are the right way up when they are being photographed) and running copy to and from the post (or the magazine or newspaper, if it is nearby).

As you progress in the department you may be allowed to put

forward your own ideas on promotion and advertising and if you understand how cost-effective it has to be, you may be successful in persuading the company to try out your idea. Promotion may involve travelling to various musical dealers and arranging for demonstrations (about which more later), standing for 12 hours a day on an exhibition stand answering questions about products (this presupposes you have learnt the answers) and generally attending all functions mounted by the company. The press reception, once a common event in the musical instrument industry, is now noted principally for its rarity. If a new instrument is to be launched, it can be a cost-effective exercise to gather up all interested journalists, radio producers, etc in one venue and show them the goods. In the old days such events were often the setting for excellent lunches with free alcohol accompaniment. The distribution companies would watch benignly as journalists became unsteady on their feet and wouldn't worry too much if their products weren't noticed. In those days they felt that the good will which was spread by the event was well worth the effort and expenditure. (As a former journalist who has, on occasion, been known to attend such an event, I often wonder whether the company concerned ever considered how much good will still existed in the scribe the following morning.)

Towards the end of the 1970s, musical instrument distributors were going bankrupt at an alarming rate. Some of them failed through bad management, some through bad luck and some through distributing bad products, and although I doubt whether any of them closed because of holding too many press parties, those which were left girded their loins, pulled in their belts and put a partial ban on such frivolities. This mood even extended to America and Germany. The major trade exhibitions, which become important events for everybody seriously trading in the musical instrument industry have, for decades, been the scenes of enormous bun fights. Lowrey give a vast champagne breakfast to thousands of dealers and press people every June and there are parties galore during February when the

The large Rose-Morris guitar repair department with its resident expert and a large assortment of guitars.

international trade meets in Frankfurt (an appalling choice of venue, incidentally). But these events are now only a pale imitation of what they used to be.

The parties which still occur tend to be very 'Hard Sell'. The thirsty journalist is likely to have to sit through an hour of 'product knowledge' (someone shouting the product's praises) before being allowed near a wine bottle. I am sure that many writers now leave the events convinced that executives of the musical instrument company may carry out spot checks at the door to see if the journalist has been paying attention.

Larger wholesalers maintain their own repair departments. Here, Adrian Legge, Rose-Morris' guitar expert, sets-up an Ovation guitar for a customer.

101

But press parties are fun to plan, hell to organise and provide every member of the advertising and promotions department with headaches. The headaches you get (if you manage to get a job in such a department) must be only those of overwork. However tempting it seems, never drink at your own parties!

If your English, art or typing isn't right for the exotic world of promotion (or if you don't fancy toadying to a pack of snotty journalists), you may have the one particular skill which all musical instrument wholesalers are looking for — you may be able to demonstrate.

Being a demonstration player is rather like being a demonstration snooker player, only you also have to be able to talk well. If you are really a virtuoso on your chosen instrument (ideally keyboards or guitar) and you don't want to trudge the boards as a pro, you might consider working to promote a particular brand of instruments. A few years ago most companies kept several full-time demonstrators on their staff who toured the country (and sometimes the world) showing off a particular guitar or keyboard range. In the last few years companies have fired many and have tended to ask such musicians to work on a freelance basis, but there is one important development which is forcing the more alert companies to reconsider the situation.

The microcomputer is revolutionising musical instruments. In simple terms, the computer is producing sounds itself and is also taking over control of existing instruments such as synthesizers. Pete Townshend has predicted that the guitar will be dead in a few years and I agree with him. The computer is everything and this has caught many of the larger wholesalers napping. New distribution companies have sprung up which sell nothing but computer-based instruments. The larger companies are now retaliating by finding their own micro instruments but they don't understand what the revolution is all about. If you do, and if

Many craftsmen still work within the discipline of guitar building and repair. This is Chris Eccleshall, one of Britain's best guitar builders and a repair-man extraordinaire.

you can play a computer-based instrument, you should try to get that message over to one of these companies. A demonstrator must understand the instrument he or she is demonstrating, but must also be able to express the understanding clearly, into a microphone on stage. If you understand computer instruments, if you can play them and explain them well (and if you look presentable) you are very likely to find a job at the moment.

There are a variety of other jobs to be had inside a musical instrument wholesale company. For a musician with an abiding love of the instruments themselves, the repair and service department can offer a delightful haven. Obviously suitable applicants must possess a knowledge of instrument technology. As discussed in the last paragraph, many instruments are becoming computer-based, but the role of the electronics repair man and designer really falls outside the scope of this book. However, the enthusiast with a love of drums, guitars, brass (or computers) may be suited to caring for the instruments.

If you are in love with instruments, but can't find a place in a musical instrument company, look around for the sort of scheme that started a few years ago in Liverpool. Called the Liverpool Youth Music Opportunities Programme, the scheme was started to offer young people a chance to learn how to repair instruments. In an attic workshop the people lucky enough to get a place in the scheme make percussion instruments for the local physically and mentally handicapped, repair old instruments and return them to their owners. They also have their own recording studio. The studio is constructed around an old console provided by a local radio station and all members of the scheme get a chance to study both the practice and theory of recording.

As must have become obvious, there is no formal path of

He couldn't play them, or even tune them, but Leo Fender was responsible for a revolution in musical instruments. Pictured here outside his Music Man factory on Fender Avenue, Fullerton, California, in a photograph taken by the author.

105

entry into the musical instrument industry (this is true of most sections of the music business). There are a few courses for instrument repairers at colleges of further education (the London College of Furniture, Newark Technical College and Merton Technical College spring to mind), but there are certainly no vocational training opportunities for people who want to work exclusively with musical instruments. The training is given on the job.

Every musical instrument wholesale company has to make a profit. If it doesn't it goes out of business. That means that the company must extract more value from each employee than the cost of keeping that person employed. The wages the employee takes home only account for about half of the cost the company has to find to keep that person employed. No matter what function you take on, it isn't a difficult calculation to work out whether you're earning your keep each week or month.

If you work in the MI business you will meet many musicians. You will meet the designers of instruments and you may even meet a few stars. It's got to be better than banking, but never forget it's a business first, and the music comes second.

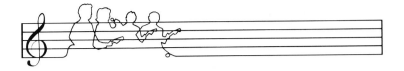

6
WORKING IN
A ROAD CREW

A 'road crew' is the body of people who support a group of musicians when they rehearse or play live 'gigs'. The road managers (or 'roadies' as they're nearly always called, no matter what their status) also help the band during recordings, television shows and private life.

Being a roadie can be a thankless and boring task, but it can also be one of the most exciting non-playing jobs in the music business. Which of the two it is depends on the roadie's temperament and on the success of the band employing him or her.

There was no such thing as a roadie before the 1960s. Some of the biggest bands used to have a few stage-hands to help musicians carry equipment and costumes, but most musicians preferred to carry their own particular instruments. The advent of high-power amplification and the transformation of the rock and roll tour into a travelling circus — complete with everything except big top — ensured that a large crew was necessary to move the organisation from town to town overnight.

There are many similarities between the old-style travelling fun fair and a successful rock band on the move. The old fairs would pick up casual labour in each town, but the specialists, the people who knew how to look after the animals and the big top, would be held on retainers, even during the months when the circus was off the road.

To read the tales of those few showmen who committed their

memories to paper, conjures up a picture of the travelling fair as an enormous, logistical exercise, with 40 caravans and 20 lorries moving from place to place each week. With the added burden of wild animals and the performers to look after, the whole thing became a nightmare and it is not surprising that this form of entertainment did not survive the dip in fortunes it suffered after the arrival of television.

But the complexity and logistical difficulties of a travelling rock band — as it erects and dismantles its elaborate lighting and sound systems, in repeating 24-hour cycles — dwarf even the achievements of the crews of the latter-day fun fairs.

The world's biggest bands may undertake 14 month world tours and in that time play in as many as 200 different halls in a dozen countries, across four continents. The job demands stamina, reliability, common sense, loyalty and skill from the roadie. In return the roadie stays in the best hotels (for the few hours he or she is allowed to sleep), travels the world and becomes 'one of the band', experiencing all the highs and lows of the stars' performances at a very close second hand.

There are many different categories of roadie, in a complex hierarchy, and the duties in various jobs differ considerably. The lowest form of roadie is usually called an 'amp roadie'. This person's job is to lug the huge amplifiers out of the trucks and set them up on the stage. The amps then have to be wired and maintained during performance. If something goes wrong with an amplifier during the concert, the amp roadie has to replace rapidly the faulty amplifier with a substitute, being as quick and as unobtrusive as possible. When the show is all over and the stars are whisked away to the champagne reception, the night-club or their beds, the amp roadie is left in the empty hall to carry all of the amplifiers out into the pouring rain and load them back onto the truck.

The specialist roadie is someone who is knowledgeable about particular types of instruments. There are 'guitar roadies', 'keyboard roadies' and 'drum roadies'. Each of these workers is responsible for their individual group of instruments and, in some of the more successful bands, each member may have his or her own personal instrument roadie. These specialists worry only about the collection of guitars, for example, and ensure that they are properly strung, in tune and in good playing condition for the night's performance, recording session or rehearsal. During the concert, the specialist roadies will crouch beside the stage observing only the instruments for which they are responsible. If something goes wrong — a string breaks or a drum head breaks — the roadie is instantly on stage offering a replacement to the musician. When musicians become stars, everything must be seen to run smoothly.

Other specialist roadies concentrate on public address systems. As well as amplifying their own instruments, most bands today own or hire huge public address systems with which to make themselves heard. PA technology has become very advanced, and it is usual for part of a crew to be devoted entirely to the erection, operation and dismantling of this system. The system will include huge PA loudspeaker 'bins', so large that it takes three people to carry one, and complex sound mixers which balance the sound which the audience will hear and balance the sound which the band themselves will hear through their monitors. The engineers who mix the sound may be integral members of the PA crew or they may be specialist sound mixers hired by the band.

Yet another group of specialists in the crew are the lighting roadies. Some bands own all of their own lights and hire their own crews to operate them, others choose to rent both lights and crew from an organisation offering this service. The lighting crew tend to work separately from the sound stage crews, but when the trucks have to be loaded, everybody pitches in.

You don't have to have *any* formal qualifications to become a roadie, but you can't become one just by asking. Roadies are people who love the music; they wouldn't be there otherwise. Many of them are musicians themselves who, for one reason or another, have sublimated their own music ambition to the service of other musicians. Some of them drift into the job; but

A stage show is a team effort. Rory Gallagher (left) is entertaining the crowds at the Montreux Festival, while off stage the sound man is listening to his talkback (headphones) and giving (or taking) instructions to lights or back line crew while controlling the show.

they either learn quickly how to do it or they're out of the crew almost as soon as they have joined.

For most roadies, the occupation is insecure — similar to being casual help in a fairground. Bands going on tour tend to pick up stage help for six weeks and pay it off at the end. Even rock'n'roll has been suffering from the recession and the days when a full crew was kept on the payroll while the band was off the road have long since disappeared. Some of the specialists are kept on between tours — usually on a reduced retainer — as their skills are too valuable to lose, but for the majority of roadies the life consists of short, highly paid, spells on tour, followed by weeks without work. Despite the drawbacks there is no shortage of applicants. The life is glamorous, provides intimacy with stars, travel, comradeship and a sense of belonging. If you're a professional roadie you're 'in the music business'.

Dave Liddle is stage manager and guitar roadie for Paul Weller, now a solo star after the break up of his internationally-successful group, the Jam. Dave joined the Jam as a guitar roadie towards the end of 1977 when the band were consolidating their early success and his story is typical of the way in which many people become roadies. Dave is a fine guitarist in his own right. He spent years in the late 1960s and 1970s working as a blues and jazz player, but although he had a lot of fun, the bands he played with failed to break into the charts. As a result, Dave found himself ageing and in need of a regular job.

'I'm old for a roadie,' admits Dave, 'you don't expect a roadie to be 37, but I love it. When I became a roadie I never thought, "it shouldn't be them on stage, it should be me." It was a case of . . . well I was quite old then, even for a roadie, although I was only 32. I just wanted to do something totally different that I had never really done before, although I had dabbled at it.

'I was lucky; somebody gave me an introduction to the tour manager, although I wasn't really looking for a job at the time. It was a friend of a friend and I went up for the interview and I found I knew the bloke very well. The Jam were just starting a six week UK tour and of course he offered me the job as guitar roadie. I had heard the Jam and I thought they were bloody awful, I really did. I thought, "Christ, if that's the state of modern music I don't want to know about it." I wasn't really at a loose end when I was offered the job, but on the other hand I realised I had never really been round England properly. So I agreed.'

Most roadies tend to be 17 or over, but there is no age bar at either end, as Dave's case proves. He brought to a highly successful young band his years of experience as a gigging guitarist and his considerable technical knowledge about guitars. But many musicians will wonder how a player manages to adapt to the subservient role of servicing guitars for younger, less experienced musicians.

'I suppose there is a frustrated musician's thing in me,' admits Dave, 'but I still play today, I haven't stopped playing and that makes it all right. It did seem a bit strange on that first Jam tour, however, because all I was doing was tuning the guitars and basses.'

Like most casual members of road crews, Dave found himself laid off after that first tour.

'After the end of the first tour I was laid off and I had a two week rest period over Christmas. I said, "Well if you want me again, you had better let me know," because I had decided to go out as a roadie with the Strawbs. Paul Weller sent a message asking me to stay with him and the band permanently.

'Bands normally pick roadies up for a tour and drop them again. It's only if roadies work out really well that they get the chance of a full-time job. It's economics that rule it today. If you're going to keep a guy permanently you're going to have to pay him a retainer when the band's not on the road and sometimes there's a lot of work during these periods and at other times there's no work at all.'

If you want to be a roadie you will have to accept that casual

113

work rarely provides for such luxuries as employment stamps and PAYE. Only the most organised managements put roadies on official payrolls and the majority insist on making weekly payments, cash in hand.

This is — of course — illegal, unless a proper self-employment contract is worked out, but the deal is often presented in such a way that you become responsible for your own tax and your own insurance contributions. The net result is that 99 per cent of casual roadies ignore both, and when they're not working they can't even draw dole money as they don't have enough paid up contributions to the National Insurance Scheme. Such arrangements are self-defeating. If you find yourself in this situation I don't anticipate that you will be able to change the way the tour management works, but it is worth your time visiting the local Social Security office and asking their advice about buying your own insurance stamps. They are never ogres if you communicate with them, they are only troublesome if you ignore them and their wretched printed forms.

Roadies can, however, earn large amounts of money.

Dave Liddle: 'How much you get as a roadie depends on how long you've been doing the job. If you're new but you know what you're doing when you go on the road with a big band you could get £150 a week plus PDs — per day expenses — and you could easily make your money up to over £200 a week. If you're experienced you can earn a lot more money. If roadies stick with a band a long time they can be earning £500 or £600 a week — they almost become part of the band.

'I know of a menial job coming up soon — a wardrobe roadie — and it pays £400 a week. Pay all depends on who the band is. That sort of pay is only for one tour, however. Then again, if you're with a very big band that tour could be a 14 month world-wide tour.

'Of course, American roadies working in the USA earn a lot more than British roadies. Five years ago, when we first went to the States, I was chatting to the crew with the Blue Oyster Cult and the lowest paid member of the crew was earning £800 a week then — and he was just sweeping the stage! There is money to be made in the business. Not many British roadies get work in the States, however. There's a thing that forces US bands to employ an American rather than a British bloke, although I do know several PA guys and lighting guys who have managed it.

'Young roadies don't do anything between tours. They try and save as much money on tour as they can and live off that. I know a very good young roadie, he's maybe 24 or 25, and he doesn't care who he works for and he's always working. He is willing to do guitars, drums or amps, anything to keep working. 'A good roadie is someone who just gets on with things, he's not frightened of doing anything. Even if he is an amp roadie, when someone asks him for help with a drum kit, he's there. It's willingness that's the first requirement. It's not necessarily what you know, it's how willing you are to have a go that counts. I'd love to have guys that don't chat a lot and just get on with it, although I never mind if somebody asks "how do you do this?" Reliability is also very important as is the ability to get up in the morning. It's a late night clear up — we're normally out of a gig by 1a.m. — and I normally go in to the next venue about 9.30 the following morning.

'After we leave the gig at 1a.m., a typical journey might be Edinburgh to Manchester. This takes about three or four hours and we usually drive it immediately. We will arrive at the hotel about 5a.m. and I'lll check everybody in.

I get to bed about 5.30a.m. and because I'm the stage manager I suppose I have to get up about 8.30a.m. I only get about three hours sleep. It becomes a bit of a joke on the road, I get very little sleep.

'The soundcheck with the Jam was usually held about 3.30 in the afternoon before a concert. For a show, the lighting guys normally get in about 9.30 and they're rigged and focussed by 2 or 2.30 and then they disappear until show time — they normally get their heads down. My boys in the stage crew used to get in at 12 o'clock for their call time. The pattern was: 9.30a.m. lights, 11a.m. PA and noon for the back line. The back line was up in an hour. Some crews all go in together, but most crews work on a rota of this type. The guys who work the hardest are the lighting guys.'

115

The lighting roadies may take small portable lighting towers with them, or they may erect large hydraulic or winched towers from which to hang lights (above and right).

The 'back line' is the line of instrument amplifiers which provide the source of amplification for the musician's instruments. These amplifiers are put up at the same time as the static instruments (keyboards and drums). The guitars and other mobile instruments will be tuned in the dressing rooms. The guitar roadie has the job of changing guitar strings, stretching the new strings until they will hold their tune and then tuning each guitar. Dave Liddle recalls working for the Strawbs in

116

the 1970s when they were using 12 different guitars during a concert, with all 12 guitars tuned differently. Despite this, Dave is modest about the skills necessary to become a guitar roadie.

'You don't need to know a great deal to become a guitar roadie for instance. If you can tune a guitar, or if you can use a tuning device or a strobe light, then you can become a guitar roadie. If you can play a bit it is an added advantage. If the musician has a 1958 Les Paul guitar worth £3,000, the guy isn't going to entrust it to you if you're not a player. He has to know that you know what you're doing with it. If you're an amp roadie it doesn't mean that you have to know how to break amps down and fix them, but it's handy to know a little bit about current or how to change a valve. You're given a stage plan by the stage manager and if you're brand new you just follow the stage plan. A new guy gets shown once or twice, after that it's up to him.
'The Japanese roadies who were provided to help us during our Japanese tours were amazing. We just showed them how our stuff went up once and they had it, every wire was right the next night.'

Travel is an attractive prospect for any young person and travelling is the principal means by which successful groups earn their money. You may have read reports in the music press about bands losing money even on successful tours — you should take such reports with a pinch of salt. Although inefficiency can sometimes cause a sell-out tour to make a loss, the only reason for putting such a circus on the road is to make money. Once a band has had a couple of hit records, the best means of exploiting the popularity is to tour. Many young people have got to know the world as members of road crews.

Dave Liddle has seen most of the developed world during his time with the Jam.

'A roadie with a big band can really see the world. I've been to Japan three times, America seven times, Europe, God knows how many times. You do get to see something of the country on a day off. If you're doing a "day off run" — such as when we travelled from Berlin to Amsterdam for example — you see a lot of the countryside, but because we'd been on the road a long time most of the guys just slept or got drunk. I just watched the country go by. One bit of country becomes like any other bit of country. It's like America. Once you've seen one state you've seen them all. The highways are all the same and if you're travelling in a coach you do get a bit bored with it. I've ended up knowing just a few streets in each city — maybe five blocks each way from the hotel we've been staying in. But there are certain places you get to know well. In New York you find that all the guitar roadies run down to Manny's, a music shop on 42nd St. You can meet all the guitar roadies in the world down there.'

'Normally any English band touring abroad will, wherever possible, take all its own personnel. The only thing they'll pick up locally will be the extra PA people who come with the PA hire company. They'll also take their own front man (sound mixer) and their own monitor man. They'll also take their own lighting director as well.

'In Japan the promotors expect to provide you with 12 or 15 extra pairs of hands to help. The only thing is that they've got a few old fashioned things out there. There's a regulation that prohibits lighting trusses from being used. They use theatre pipes and if you have to change a light pattern you've got to do it on theatre pipes and it is hilarious to watch. Every light has to be moved and focussed by people with long bamboo sticks. But they're very good at it, very fast.'

I mentioned earlier in this chapter that there are some female roadies. Unfortunately, they are few in number. When they start in the job, roadies are expected to hump huge amplifiers about and some of these are so heavy that only the biggest men prove up to the task. The jobs which go to women tend to be wardrobe roadie, make up artists or tour manager (rather a different job to a roadie's).

However, I have met half-a-dozen girls who, despite their frail looks, can handle a bass amplifier with the best of the lads. If you're female and you think you would enjoy this uncomfortable but exciting life, you stand a better chance now of getting a roadie's job than ever before.

The problem for all new, professional roadies is finding work. After finishing a tour a roadie needs to have another period of work lined up and only a constant look out for opportunities will keep the offers coming in.

> Dave Liddle: 'Whenever a roadie is travelling he will be meeting other bands who might offer him work. When we were in New York a temporary member of our crew went along to see Dave Edmunds. Dave asked him when he would be finished with us and he was invited to go out with them the week after we finished our tour. Everybody needs a week or so off after a tour, but it can be difficult to keep work regular unless you're versatile.'

A roadie works very hard on tour and needs a break after the marathon. During the tour the road crew are either setting up, breaking down or travelling. Some members of the crew manage to snatch sleep in the bus, others can't. This long period of insomnia is interspersed with periods of either great physical activity or crushing boredom. The high spots are the performances.

> 'The worst thing about being a roadie for me isn't all the night driving,' explains Dave, 'it's loading up in the pouring rain. You also get your hours broken up and you feel slightly out of it all. On the other hand the best thing is seeing the show work perfectly. You see the show every night of the week, but you still get a real buzz when it works well.'

Becoming a roadie demands that you start as an amateur and learn something about bands, their equipment and the way the business works. You do your apprenticeship (largely unpaid) with unsuccessful local bands who can't afford to offer more than a few drinks and a pound or so towards expenses. Dave has watched many youngsters start:

120

'If you want to get in you have to hang about bands, you do a little bit for them. You go to a few gigs and say "Can I help you load up?" and get to know people and it's basically that; it progresses from there. You start with the no-name band and go on to better bands. Perhaps the band you start with will make it. If you've got a driving licence it's even handier because you can drive for them. I think that's important — although I haven't got one. If you know a little bit about the gear and you offer to set it up for a local band it's very helpful and sometimes you rub shoulders with very good musicians. You can't just say "I want to be a roadie" to yourself, you've got to be prepared to say it to bands and you've got to be in the right place at the right time. Of course, the bigger the band the more specialised you've got to be.

'It's useful if you can learn a lot about instruments but it's not really necessary. I can re-wire guitars, repair them and, if I put my mind to it, build them. But that's not really necessary. I pass a lot of repair and maintenance work on to specialists. But I have mended broken necks many times on the road. You've got to be good with your hands to be a roadie.

'If you want to know a lot of other roadies there are pubs they go to, there are little cliques of roadies. I don't make a practice of knowing other roadies because I think that when I've finished work, I've finished work.

'There's two types of roadie in the business, a good roadie and a bad one. A good one will say "yeah sure I'll do all that, fine" and a bad one will say "Oh, that's not my job, I'm not doing that." Now and again that attitude persists if they're allowed to get away with it. Sometimes the seed of unwillingness is sown by someone who advises them not to do something or else they'll always be lumbered with it or he says "if you do that, they'll have us all doing it".'

Although Dave cheerfully admits to being older than the average roadie, there are many avenues of promotion open for those who are ambitious enough to explore them. Dave started as a skilled specialist looking after guitars and was promoted to stage manager (although he retained responsibility for the guitars). Stage manager is a job which calls for considerable

121

organisational ability as well as specialist knowledge.

'The stage manager's job entails looking after the crew, making sure that the gear goes up on time, making sure that the dimensions of the stage are correct, making sure that the lighting rig is right and so on. He's given a list of all the dates, times and hotels by the tour manager and then once he's got the list of gigs he has to 'front' them. That means visiting the venues in advance if he doesn't know them. Even if I know the venue I still prefer to get the promotors to send through a stage plan which will show the dimensions, the position and type of power outlets, the clearances for flying lights from the roof, details about whether we can chain-hoist lights up or whether we need ground supports. The stage manager will also need information about stage heights and he will have to make sure there is a barrier in front of the stage where it is needed. Out on the road his job is to get the guys in the road crew up in the morning. The tour manager looks after the band. Some big crews have both road crew bosses and stage manager. The stage manager has to get them to the gig, make sure the gig is running all right, make sure there are no problems and this extends even to arranging what dinner times the crew will take.'

Attention to detail is a vital part of both a stage manager's and a roadie's job. If the band turn up at a gig without an important connecting cable — well, it just mustn't happen!!

If you think you are built to be a roadie — physically and mentally — work with local bands until you get your first professional job. You'll have a great deal of fun, but you'll also do a lot of very hard work.

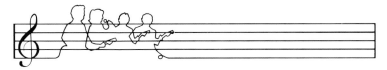

7

WORKING IN
POP GROUP MANAGEMENT,
AGENCY AND
MUSIC PUBLISHING

How do you fancy sitting behind a big desk with a huge cigar in your mouth and a phone in each hand on which you talk simultaneously to record companies in Los Angeles and Sydney? To complete the picture add rows of gold albums on the wall, alongside signed photographs of the stars, and white leather couches which squat on even-whiter carpets.

If that's what you think pop group management is all about, think again. There are a *few* managers and agents who work in this style, but the majority occupy crummy rooms above corner shops, even when they're representing successful pop groups.

Management and agency is something you can set up in yourself, as I did in the late 1960s. Your chances of being successful depend upon your resilience, your aggression and the amount of money you've got to start with. I flew high for a few years and then crashed to the ground; I hadn't got enough capital to tide me over the bad times. I was only 19 when I started and the way the music business has gone in the last few years, teenage managers are as acceptable now as they were in the 1960s.

It isn't possible to start up as a music publisher on your own without first building a base of recording artists or songwriters. Publishing is rather different to both management and agency and will be dealt with at the end of this chapter.

So how do you manage a pop group? You ask a small pop group to let you be their manager. But even local pop groups are sophisticated these days and they're likely to tell you to sling your hook, unless you can offer them something they need. What every struggling band needs more than anything else (except money) is paid work. There are always ten bands chasing one gig and the would-be manager who can say 'I've got a booking for you' will certainly be taken seriously.

Before getting into details of how to break into this sub-world, it's worth examining the set-up of the business. In the last chapter I described the work carried out by the crew which a successful band uses on the road. But the entire machine is governed by a management and agency office. 20 years ago, management and agency were entirely separate functions: managers controlled artists' careers, agents found them work. This structure still holds for the very biggest stars, but for many the roles are undertaken by the same office.

Until a band has a big hit, the struggle is to find enough of the right sort of work which will keep the band living and which will help to build a club following. It is also important to ensure that the band plays in the right sort of places where they are likely to be noticed by record company staff and radio and TV producers.

For a local band, the difficulty is in getting any sort of work. In the 1960s local bands were paid £15 a night for a three hour performance. In the 1980s they're getting £25 a night. The bands are effectively paying club owners for the privilege of playing.

Breaking out of this vicious circle depends on two things, the quality of the band and the aggression and tenacity of the management. It must be realised that good management is of the utmost importance to a band's career. For those bands lucky enough to be signed to a successful and established manager, the

124

situation should improve immediately as the manager uses his or her muscle to get them appearances in support of more successful acts, but a band signed to an agent or manager as small as themselves will be lucky to survive the experience.

There are two courses open to a would-be agent or manager. The first is to join the staff of an established office, the second is to go it alone. The first offers the chance of paid experience, the second demands that you pay to get the experience. It is possible that if you go it alone you will make it big. Andrew Loog Oldham was one of many who made it from nothing in the 1960s, Malcolm Maclaren made it in the 1970s and a host of new managers have emerged in the early 1980s. It's for you to choose the path which suits you (or which is open to you).

If you decide you would like the security of working in an established agent's or manager's office you will need to know something about the duties which would be required of you. There aren't many 'agency only' operations left in the rock'n'roll business, although agencies still flourish in mainstream show business, but if you joined an agent's office as a school leaver, the chances are you would do so to become a 'junior booker'.

One of London's most successful agents is Barry Dickens. He started as a tea boy/junior booker in the office of the all-powerful Harold Davidson in the 1960s and during the 1970s rose to become a director of MAM, the organisation which has, in its time, managed and represented such artists as Tom Jones, Engelbert Humperdinck, Gilbert O'Sullivan and Rick Wakeman. Despite his directorship, Barry hankered to return to his roots and three years ago he opened his own agency in partnership with another well-established agent. The agency is called International Artists and it operates out of plush offices in Soho's Wardour Street in London.

Today he acts as both promotor and agent, booking venues like Wembley, to promote stars such as Neil Young, as well as maintaining a careful look-out for promising young bands. From time to time he employs school leavers to work in the agency as junior bookers and he knows what he wants.

125

'When I am employing a youngster I am looking for someone who's hungry . . . hungry for business and life,' explains Barry. They probably have to beat my door down, it's a very small business and it's very hard to get in to. If someone writes a lot of letters to me they've got a better chance of getting an interview than someone who writes only one.

'I think presentation of application letters is important and applicants really need to live within an hour of the office. There's no formula for the type of person we are looking for, they need to be aggressive at times and charming at others. They should be reasonably articulate and be someone who knows what he wants out of life. The person must know that he wants to be successful and understand that he's got to work for it.

Like most of the music business, the offices of managers and agents are almost exclusively staffed by male executives and, with the exception of secretaries, the very few females who operate in the field tend to be managers rather than agents.

'There aren't many women agents . . . in the US there's Sue Menges who's the biggest film agent in the States. There's a few female managers. There's nothing against them in the agency world, it's just very very hard. For a girl it's a lot harder than for a guy. If I employed a girl I think she'd have to be a secretary first . . . I don't think that's a chauvinist statement, because girls are prepared to be secretaries and boys aren't. Secretaries get to see precisely how somebody works. In the William Morris agency in America, one of the biggest agencies in the world, male agents all have to become secretaries first, that's how they start. They start in the mail room and from there they graduate to being a secretary. They're taking dictation, answering phone calls and learning the business.'

Perhaps another reason why there are so few women agents is because the need for aggression is a constantly recurring theme and as it is men who do the hiring, girls have trouble in convincing them of their aggression. The main talent an agent is looking for in a new recruit is the ability to sell acts to promotors.

'There does need to be a little bit of aggression in an applicant. I don't mean he's got to go and punch somebody in the mouth, I'm not looking for that. You can succeed with charm sometimes. With certain people you can be charming and it'll work, other people need someone aggressive to attack them. We need someone who can adapt to the circumstances and the people they're dealing with.'

Selling acts on the telephone can be as soul-destroying as selling double glazing or life insurance and only the strong survive. The salesperson is in the position of being an actor, not only with the people he or she is selling to, but with the artists on whose behalf they are acting.

Barry Dickens: 'You've always got to consider what artists want to hear from you. I've lost acts through telling them the truth and being totally normal, and they've later turned round and told me the reason they haven't signed with me is that I haven't come on strong enough.

There are now very few good gigs available, even for the best bands. In the heyday of the pop business every Top Rank or Mecca hall was booking bands, but many of these clubs are now bingo palaces and the pubs, which for a few years in the 1970s provided a useful alternative, are now also turning their backs on live music. In the early days, agents would act for hundreds of bands. Today, it is changed.

'Years ago we felt we could do anything . . . we used to sign hundreds of bands. Maybe three of them would make it . . . it was a case of slinging enough mud against the wall to make some stick. Now we only go after bands we think have got a good shot at making it and that means that every act we represent is important to us. There's not the room for a new booker to experiment and learn that there used to be.

'When I'm interviewing people for a junior booker's job I am looking for common sense. It's got nothing to do with examination results, you've either got it or you haven't. I'm the only

127

person in my office who didn't go to university or college, but that doesn't matter at all. The university graduate has shown that he has the ability to learn and that's important, but he may or may not, have common sense. I also consider how somebody dresses to be very important. I'm not saying they've got to wear pin stripe suits, but they've got to be reasonably smart, well turned out, even if it's casual. I don't want somebody coming in who doesn't take any pride in the way they look. I don't mind if people come for jobs in jeans and a T-shirt, but I think they should be clean and I think they should look nice, because if they work here they'll be representing our artists as well as us.

'It is very hard to say whether I'd take a university graduate over a comprehensive leaver, it depends on the individual. I'm looking for someone who wants to succeed. Sometimes a university graduate will come in and think he has a right to a job just because he has become a Bachelor of Science or whatever it is. Some of them think they're geniuses and that I should automatically employ them, but that's not necessarily the case. We've had quite a few university graduates start here who don't work here any more!'

As Barry Dickens explains, joining an agent as a junior booker doesn't grant the right to ring up David Bowie and offer him seven nights at Earl's Court.

'They've all got to do some kind of apprenticeship. I like people to start at about 18. They have to be presentable, know about music and be up with what is happening today. It would not be enough for them to just enjoy music, most people just enjoy music, I'm looking for someone who wants to look on it as a business.

'A beginner would start by making the tea, running the messages and, hopefully, by *listening*. That's the way I started. If they keep their mouths shut and listen they will get involved in things; going round the clubs and meeting people. This is a business about meeting people and that's why they've got to look presentable. After they've done a bit of that I would give them small acts to start booking.

'They would start by filling up date sheets for smaller artists.

They'd have to hustle venues . . . they'd become a booker. The way they hustle venues is by ringing the promotor, telling him about the band and asking him to book them. The promotor probably won't have heard of the band and the good booker will tell him why he should try the band out. If they can't sell the band to him it's got to be phone down and on to the next one. It's persistence that counts. There's a big difference between a booker and an agent. The booker is told by the agent "in the month of May I need 20 dates for XYZ band." The booker will book the dates for me. The difference is that the agent has to be more creative because the booker will come back and say "this is what I've done." The agent works out if it makes sense: whether the dates are too far apart, is that date a good idea for their career? It's not always money that decides the right dates, an agent has to develop an artist's career. To do that sometimes it may mean accepting less money in order to play the right place. The only reason that the wrong place will offer you more money is that they know they're the wrong place.

'The business is a lot harder now than it was, just because there are less places to book. When I started, there were pubs on every street corner that were booking bands, but they all went out of business because the bands started asking too much. They're all discos now.

'It takes a thick skin to be a successful booker. It probably takes 20 calls before making a sale, and selling is what it's all about. It's like selling baked beans . . . it's a product and the fact the product happens to be a pop group is irrelevant.

'There isn't any training course available, the training comes from sitting around and listening. We have an office with three people in it and they're on the phone all the time. They learn their job in that office. Junior bookers get on the phone themselves and if they get into trouble with a venue they've got experienced people to turn to.

'Bookers graduate to becoming an agent naturally after they've been booking successfully for a while. If the booker starts to show promise we can spot them and we move them up from booking a £50-a-night group to booking a £100-a-night band, which is not quite so easy. At that level the band may have had a semi-hit and they may give the booker a harder time. Then a rising booker would move up to a £300-a-night act and then to a £500 and so on. Once you're at £1,000-a-night you're away. That sort of act can pull 1,000 people in and the agent who is booking them is beginning to learn.

'The booker has to learn all this, and that probably takes a couple of years. Of course we're only talking about booking in Britain. Then there's the rest of the world to learn about.'

Barry Dickens makes the role of the agent sound tough, but for the applicant who accepts that the music business is a *business* and proves he or she can sell, the rewards can be considerable.

'It's not easy to say how much a booker will earn, it all depends how successful they are. The way I work it is that somebody has to earn five times what I pay them. I have to have an income that brings me £25,000 if I am to pay them £5,000 a year. When you get to £10,000 a year it works out about four times the annual salary.

'The right person at 20-years-old can earn £25,000 a year, if they can book enough to earn £100,000 worth of commission a year, and they can make a lot of money.

'We contract our young people, once they've shown they're going to work out, and it's a bit like an apprenticeship. When they first start they get a six months contract and then it builds up. But you can't stop people leaving. There's always a temptation for a young booker, who finds himself with a hit artist, to leave and set up on his own, but it's true to say that agents and managers are generally around a lot longer than artists. It's no good getting just one hit act which you handle. You've got to have one hit act that you build into two which becomes three and so on.

'It's a tough business. When things go wrong you don't get a week's notice, you go on the spot. It's a business, that's what people don't understand. Everybody involved in the business has to make a profit. Once anybody on the staff isn't making a profit, the agent's not making a profit.

'I expect a young person working here to be out in the clubs every night of the week looking for new acts. This is a very competitive business. Record companies have people out, agents have people out and you've got to spot the acts you think are good and you have to spot them before anybody else.

'I still like to see a band live before we take them on. The recording studio can hide a lot of sins. Our business is live work, if a band can't reproduce their sound on stage they're no good to us.'

Most management companies also act as agent for their artists, the reason being economics. Agents earn 10 per cent or 15 per cent from each booking they arrange. Managers typically earn 25 per cent gross of all the artist's income. Some managers even add an agency fee to this and for the combined services of management and agency, the company may take 30 per cent or even 35 per cent. The young person joining a management office of this type would find the early work very similar to the junior booker's role as described by Barry Dickens, but the junior joining a pure management company would have other duties.

For a management office to be able to afford the hire of junior help, they must already have at least one successful artist. Once an artist is successful the amount of looking-after he, she or they require suddenly becomes considerably more than the help required when they were unsuccessful. This is not simply because the number of engagements increases dramatically, it is also because success may have a very unpleasant effect on an artist's ego, and the artist will demand that 'their office' does everything from booking dates to arranging the employment of nannies for their children. This reliance on 'the office' proves very attractive for newly-rich young people and for a while it must seem to them as though every annoyance in life has been removed. If they want a new car, the office will find it. If they want a new house, the office will find it. In some cases the office also becomes the source of lovers. Providing such services often falls to junior assistants in a star's management offices and although fun, I am told that it rapidly becomes depressing: rather like dancing for an ungrateful emperor. A situation in

131

which a young person suddenly earns a lot of money allows unscrupulous managers to steal from artists. All of the stories you have heard about crooked managers in the music business are true and you can add 50 per cent to all estimates of corruption.

The situation that occurs once an attractive young person is given fame and money at the same time prevents all but the tiniest minority from keeping a careful eye on the flow of their money. I have watched helplessly as established managers weeded out alert young musicians from potentially successful bands for the very reason that they might not succumb to the flattery and adulation that stardom brings and might block the manager's attempt to purloin a major part of the band's income. 'Smart musicians need not apply!'

Having painted a dark picture, it is fair to say that some management offices are honest and businesslike. But the attitude remains the same. The star is allowed to jump from his Rolls Royce into his yacht — complaining all the way — while the 'man from the management' has to worry about parking the car and paying the mooring fees. Managers often take on the role of baby-sitters. The fact that some of the sweets are stolen from the baby shouldn't surprise anyone.

It was as a reaction to such horrors that many of the successful new bands have firmly resisted a move to London and have also resisted the lure of plush-carpet management and promises of film parts. Many of the new bands choose to stick with their provincial managers and ensure that accountants watch every penny. But human nature doesn't change and I'm sad to report that several well-known acts have already changed their minds and have succumbed to the lure of the big city.

In defence of the professional managers, they do have the international contacts and abilities which can transform a one-hit-wonder into an international star, a feat that is extremely difficult and which cannot be achieved by talent alone. Many survivors in the business look back on the days of the management 'rip-off' as a dues-paying period and accept the fact that if it were not for the missing millions, they wouldn't be in the position of being able to earn any millions at all. That is the balanced view. Some famous musicians never recover from the shock of learning that the house they live in doesn't belong to them, the car they drive is hired and that the Inland Revenue really does mean it when it says 'you owe us £50,000'.

Joining an established management office won't automatically turn you into a crook. You will learn more in a year about the business than you would in five years on the fringes and you will have most of your illusions about the business shattered. You will be in an excellent position to consider setting yourself up as a manager, but surprisingly few junior management staff take this step. I believe that this is because their insight into large-scale professional management shows them just how much money is involved and how risky it can be.

Those who have never worked in professional management are much more inclined to set up on their own: they don't know the size of the difficulties and are therefore not put off. It is these people who succeed most often.

It need not take much money to start as a manager, but it takes a reserve of money to see you through the bad times. After you've promised a talented, but undiscovered, band that you can find them work and turn them into stars you are faced with a problem — how are you going to finance the operation. Many managers start from their bedroom and use their mum's phone. If they are very, very good at getting work for the band, this may be enough. But once a band thinks they've got management, they want to be looked after. When they want to hire a van, it's their manager they ask to find the deposit — 'just until we get paid'. If an instrument blows up, or if a new instrument is needed, it's the manager who is asked to find the money or sign the HP guarantee form. Don't do the latter, no matter how much you believe in the band. The band member may leave, be run over or be put in prison and you will find yourself paying for an instrument you don't want and, in some cases, don't possess.

The more money you have, the more money you will pour

'The deal is signed!' The author as manager (centre, standing) with members of The Expence and record-producer Andy Black at Polydor Records, 1968.

into the band you believe in. It is a trap which has ruined many moderately successful dads as they proudly watched their off-spring making unusual noises with a saxophone or synthesizer. It's a great temptation for them to set up as manager, provide the funds for decent amplification and transport and then wait for the band to turn into Musical Youth or the Jam. It doesn't happen — at least, not very often. Dad will be the wrong age group to make a good manager unless he's a music business professional and, even if the band are good, he'll end up losing the act to a more experienced manager, or, more likely, losing his money as he watches the band break up in disillusionment.

Not surprisingly, bands like to record. Recording costs money and it's the manager's job to find it. In the 1960s penniless managers could establish themselves on nothing (as I did) and live by the seat of their pants, always betting that Saturday's gig commission would be paid before the phone was cut off. In the 1970s this became impossible as the finance needed to put even the smallest band on the road was colossal. In the early 1980s, the wheel has turned full circle and penniless managers are again promoting small bands with the 'co-operative' element to the fore again. Today, many small bands regard their manager as one of the group and would be likely to distrust him or her if they had any money. Their lack of success is almost their guarantee of honesty, much as it was in the 1960s, and, wherever possible, successful bands hang onto their small-time managers. Some managers are able to grow with the situation, others are not, and many bands have seen their promising careers wither away as their less-than-capable management have tried to cope with the stresses of early success and high finance.

If you want to be a pop group manager, the best advice I can give is to go out and do it. You don't need a single, formal qualification. You do need to be tough and you do need to be alert. To get anywhere you need to be bossy and you need to be able to tell a good band from a bad one. Too much loyalty, especially to a mediocre member of a band, will inhibit both your growth and the band's and all the unpleasant tasks, from

135

sacking that original, but flagging, band member, to asking a bruiser on a dance hall door for the gig money, will fall on your shoulders. It's great fun.

Music publishers *are* at the traditional heart of the music business. At one time, they ran the business and even the record companies courted them. Today it has changed and publishers have become royalty collection agencies first and publishers second.

Before the advent of good record players, the only way for the public to enjoy music was to play it themselves. For most this required the purchase of sheet music. Half a century ago publishers occupied the position of dominance now enjoyed by the record companies. A hit would sell few records, but would sell upwards of 100,000 copies of the sheet music. Today, even a number 1 song sells only a few thousand copies of the sheet music.

For this reason, publishers are no longer interested in publishing: they are interested in owning the copyright to songs. Some publishers still operate on the system of finding a good song and then trying to interest a well-known performer to record it. If this happens, and if the record is a hit, the owner of the publishing rights (and the composer) will often make far more money from the situation than the hit performer. Really good songs just go on and on earning money long after the original hit version has been forgotten.

Many publishers, however, merely act as collecting agencies working on behalf of certain management companies or artists. When a song is recorded someone has to get the publishing rights and more and more artists, both established and new, are deciding that it might as well be their own company. Many publishing companies exist which only service the songs written by one, or perhaps two, songwriters.

If the idea of working in publishing appeals to you, you will have to apply to work in one of the largest and most established publishing houses who still represent songwriters as a separate entity to recording artists. Such companies are listed in *Kemps*

136

Music Yearbook which is kept at larger public libraries. Juniors, male or female, will inevitably have to suffer the apprenticeship of clerical work, but they will discover how the songwriting industry works. If you are lucky enough to get work in a music publisher's office, the ultimate ambition must be either to 'buy' or 'sell' songs — often people do both. The 'buyer' listens to the thousands of songs which arrive each year and is looking for that little something that makes a song a hit. Of course, nobody really knows what that 'little something' is — not even those who are most successful at finding it. The 'seller' has to persuade recording artists, producers and managers that the songs they are peddling have that 'little something'. It's a job of contacts, and there's no way to start other than by becoming a junior in a large office.

Because music publishing has changed so much, there are very few openings for those who want to work just in publishing. Many publishers have been managers, agents or producers and have drifted into the publishing role by circumstance. Very often the role becomes almost indistinguishable from other management activities in the music business, but it is every bit as enjoyable.

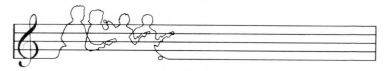

8

WORKING ON
THE FRINGES OF
THE MUSIC BUSINESS

For every star who appears on television in *Top of the Pops* there are 20 people employed to keep him or her there. The star needs a manager, an agent, a road crew, a publicist, a designer, a make-up and hair artist, a record producer, a sound engineer, a photographer, an instrument supplier, an instrument repairer, music publishers, a lawyer, an accountant and a bank manager.

Some of these occupations have been described in earlier chapters, but the rest of these pursuits are best described as being on the 'fringe' of the music business.

Leaving aside 'professional' help from lawyers, accountants and bankers, every successful star needs a publicist, a designer, a photographer and a video director. The designers usually work in many fields and treat music business clients as merely one of the many types of prima donna to be catered for. Most video directors produce pop promotional videos as a means to some other form of film making. There is a small school of specialist pop video houses who are producing nothing but music videos, but although these workers probably regard themselves as being in the music business, they are, quite rightly, primarily concerned with making video images rather than promoting a pop star.

The pop publicist, however, is firmly in the music business. The publicist is both a figure of fun and someone to be feared, despite the fact that they often seem simply pathetic. Publicists have a thankless task, but their offices are fun to work in and provide a vital insight into the workings of the music business. There are two main functions undertaken by the publicist: the first is to try and get their lesser-known clients written about, the second is to try and stop stories being written about their most famous clients. It seems a contradiction, but it clearly reveals the impact of stardom on the individual.

Most, but not all, pop publicists are ex-music paper journalists. Despite this, two of the most successful London publicists have never put a pen to paper but have entered the business from other areas. Until a couple of years ago it seemed that every pop publicist had to be in London. There's been a slight shift away as some bands (the Human League for example) have resisted the traditional move to the capital which usually follows stardom, and many managers and publicists have followed this lead and asserted their individuality by remaining in the provinces. I believe that this will be a short-lived phenomenon. The convenience of meeting people in London is undoubted. There are other sorts of convenience: all of the national newspapers and music papers are based in London and the need to get photographs 'over by bike' must outweigh the idea of sending them by first class post from Edinburgh.

Pop publicists are the middle men who 'front' the world on behalf of the artist. Many musicians and music business journalists regard them as parasites, but they are vital to the functioning of the business. The 'parasite' view develops because publicists are available for hire by almost anybody. If you can find the weekly £200 to £500 to pay for a publicist's services, his or her office (unlikely to be the principal publicist) will jump through the hoop in an attempt to get your name into the papers. Very few publicists turn down the chance to represent any act.

The procedure is simple. Once a band or singer is signed for a record release, it is in the interest of all concerned for the artist to

139

be written about in the newspapers and covered in the broadcasting medium in as much detail as possible. The management of the artist or band visits the publicist and hires him or her to act for them, usually for a period of six weeks (two weeks before the release date of the record and four weeks afterwards). The publicist meets the artist and discusses how to present the best image. Image has become everything in the last couple of years and many artists are now more concerned with developing the right image for the media than with their music. If a promotional video is being made then the publicist will probably take his or her image lead from the image developed for the video. Still photographs will be taken (more about the photographers later), a biography will be concocted (rarely accurate) and a plan of campaign will be worked out. The publicist is charged with the job of ensuring that as many newspapers as possible write about the new artist and his or her record. But how can they guarantee this? The answer is that they can't, although some of them have become sufficiently powerful to be almost able to guarantee it. A publicist gains power by becoming known as a good source of stories and by providing 'exclusives' by which every paper lives. Although it must seem to the hopeful artist that getting into the papers is an impossible thing, many reporters and sub-editors see the filling of blank pages as being equally hard. They're never short of news, but they're often short of the right kind of news. This is where the pop publicist comes in. If the showbiz pages of a national paper regularly carry pictures of an up-and-coming star they've got to pick the right one. The well-known publicist who assures them that Band X is a winner, solves their problem (provided Band X is getting coverage elsewhere: 'coverage elsewhere' is the fail-safe every sub-editor looks for when justifying the carrying of a story). The method has a 'knock-on effect and by telling white lies, the publicist can ensure that several papers carry the story and all are happy that they've covered the 'happening' band.

But no publicist can ring an editor and just ask him or her to write about an act, no matter how friendly the publicist may be

140

with the editor. An angle must be found that convinces the newspaper person that there's a story to be told. In the boom years of pop the 'angle' was everything and, as in the golden days of Hollywood, the best publicists were those who came up with an angle which would ensure newspaper coverage. The angle still matters, and even the biggest names resort to such tactics when it suits them. Pink Floyd floated an inflatable pig over Battersea Power Station to publicise a new album a few years ago and, sure enough, it made most of the papers and got some national, peak-time TV coverage.

Publicists quiz new clients about their background, the lyrics to the song, their aspirations, their deformities, in fact about anything which will allow the publicist to develop an angle. *New artist releases new record* is no story. *Son of Falklands hero records first record* is. So is *Discovered in the typing pool* and *Dave says "I'm bi-sexual and I don't care."*

If there is no natural story to be extracted from the artists (and there usually is), publicists make one up. That's their job. They then write a press release around the theme, have just the right pictures taken (for which there is always an extra, hefty, charge) and begin to do their thing. In an earlier chapter I mentioned the tireless work of the record pluggers, and when it is realised that their efforts combine behind the scenes with the efforts of publicists, agents and managers, it will be seen just how great (and expensive) the effort has to be to establish a successful new act.

All publicists represent successful acts. The publicist who only represents new acts must either make one of them successful very rapidly, or go out of business. The job of a pop publicist has become more sophisticated in the last ten or twelve years. There is now an element of media manipulation in the role and this started at the beginning of the 1970s. The biggest rock stars discovered that they could easily become over exposed; newspapers and TV would use their face over and over again until the public was sick of it. The result was a sudden absence of the face and many faces never reappeared. The smarter stars realised that saying 'no' to requests for interviews would actually increase the desire for information, both on the part of the media and the public. As a result, stars now follow a pattern of undergoing a period around the release of a record or film when they will suffer interviews by almost anyone, and long periods of absolute silence when they will see nobody. But such manipulation has to be handled well if the media hounds aren't going to give up the chase and look somewhere else.

Every so often the most important hound must be fed an 'exclusive' out of season story in order to keep the media appetite whetted and the pot of public awareness simmering. Stars and publicists often get this wrong and the press react by refusing to carry interviews when the star needs them. The long term survivors tend to be those most adept at manipulating the media. These are the rules the publicity game works by, and if it seems strange that journalists are prepared to be manipulated in this way, it will come as no surprise that they sometimes rebel. This has happened in a similar game which is conducted between Buckingham Palace and the press. A similar 'close season' is controlled by the Palace, but in frustration at such manipulation, some members of the press have deliberately broken the rules in an attempt to abolish them altogether.

If you think the world of the pop publicist sounds exciting, you're right, it is. The publicist has very close contact with the stars and becomes a vital member of the management team. The most successful publicists are powerful in their own right and wield a certain respect among their anti-colleagues in the media.

You can't set up on your own as a pop publicist unless you know people. You either need to be set up by a well-known act to work in this capacity, or you must know your way around the media. Most publicists have started by becoming a junior helper in an established publicist's office and then striking out on their own.

Like all branches of the ever-attractive music business, it is not easy to get a job in a publicist's office. Those who are likely to get one are those who ask most persistently and those who are most charming. Charm is the name of the publicity game and if you can't charm the birds from the trees, forget it. Publicists suffer every kind of abuse, from reporters who can't get in to see a star, to a star who doesn't want to see reporters. The publicist must smile at all times. The person who readily loses their temper is not suited to the job. Only if you are good at pouring oil on troubled waters and if you are outgoing and thick-skinned should you chain yourself outside a publicist's office and beg for a job.

A rhino-like hide is required, for the task of attempting to introduce yourself to famous stars and powerful media people, when there is no one there to introduce you. A thick skin is also required for telling the most outrageous lies while keeping a straight face. Publicists always get the dirty end of the spade and they most often use it for shovelling a very common commodity. When someone has to be sent in to face an irate star, it's the publicist who is nominated for the job; this applies equally when it is an irate manager, TV producer or newspaper editor.

There are as many openings for women as for men in pop publicity offices, although as publicists men outnumber women ten-to-one. One publicist I know regularly employs pretty American girls who don't have British work permits. They're paid tiny sums, cash in hand, at the end of each week and their duties are to welcome the stars and the journalists to the office with a big smile, make the coffee, do the filing and generally decorate the place. When the girls begin to ask persistently about legal regular employment or when they get work permit problems they are invited to move on. There is an endless supply of such talent and that publicist is one of the most successful in London.

Most publicists run small, but properly organised offices and this field is one where office juniors really can learn the foundations of a career. Small offices are the best place to learn anything, but in the music business, the pace is so hectic that quite enormous tasks are often thrown at the most junior members of staff. It isn't easy to discover where all the publicists are, as there

143

is no central listing and no classification in the yellow pages for the profession. Some record companies will give you the information, and observation of the music press for the names of publicists will allow you to build up a file. Write and explain why you want to work in a publicist's office. The best reason is that you think you could succeed as a publicist and want to learn the ropes. When you are asked why you think you could succeed the best answer must be to suggest you have the right personality. You must enjoy meeting people, if you're not gregarious the job isn't for you. Also, it is useful if you are good at English and can write in reasonable style. Typing is also helpful.

Assuming you do persuade a publicist to give you a job, you can expect to do anything and everything. You'll certainly make the tea or coffee whether you're male or female and I'm pleased to say that publicity offices don't divide work as 'suitable for boys' and 'suitable for girls'. You'll file pictures and run out for sandwiches, but you'll also attend photographic sessions and you'll visit newspaper offices. If you prove to have a pleasant phone manner, show that you always remember messages and always 'follow through' (meaning that you always do what you say you'll do — put a photograph in the post *that* night, for example), you will quickly be allowed to work in a publicist's capacity on smaller acts handled by the office. Getting to know the newspaper journalists is half the battle in the world of publicity, and this isn't too hard as music writers regularly visit publicist's offices or meet publicist's staff at gigs. How you get on with the writers depends on you and that's why personality is such an important factor in a publicist's career.

The object of the exercise is to build up a relationship until the time comes when you can ring up 'Penny' on *The Weekly Screamer* and tell her that you've just taken on an unbelievably good band that she ought to be writing about. If she accepts your invitation to see the band, you're on your way. You can't win friendship by fawning or crawling; journalists are, in the main, bright people who react against sycophants, and the best publicists are those who are genuinely likeable people.

You will have to write some press handouts, but this is a diminishing role which has largely been taken over by the publicity departments of the record companies. At one time most of the people entering pop publicity were ex-journalists — and it still remains a refuge for some writers who leave the music press in a state of confusion after musical fashions change and leave them high and dry. Few journalists are happy to join a publicity office, however, as they would rather be free to write their stories than hustle others to do so.

One young ex-colleague of mine left an advertisement department of a weekly music paper, joined a publicist as an assistant and within two years had founded his own publicity business. That business is now five years old and represents some of the brightest of the new music stars. He set up when many of the new names were looking for publicists who weren't tired and jaded and his abilities helped him to make a name for himself. Publicity is one area where only ability counts, and if you've got it, you need never worry about your examination passes, your accent or your background. You'll be a huge success. The only drawback to the career is that it rarely leads to other things. A few publicists have gone on to become record company executives, but most stay on as independent operators until they have made enough money to retire.

Photography always seems a popular choice of career for unqualified school leavers. Few gain entrance to the profession and even fewer become photographers in their own right. Many of those who do, switch career as they pass 30.

Pop photography is such a specialised form of photography that it can legitimately be considered as belonging to the music business. There are half-a-dozen specialist pop photographers in London and if you fancy becoming one, you've not only got to prove yourself to be an excellent photographer, you've also got to save some money against the day when you will want to set up on your own.

Liking pop music isn't a good enough reason to become a pop

photographer, but a twin liking for photography and music may well be. Most photographers start off by taking pictures and submitting them to journals in the hope that they will be accepted for publication. But in the music business things work a little differently.

There are two types of photography in the music business, the planned studio session and the 'live' shot.

Some photographers manage to combine both forms and run a studio in London at which they take formal sessions, while in the evenings they travel the country to gigs and take the live performance shots. Most, however, specialise in only one area. If you're an amateur photographer who would like to take action shots at pop concerts you won't get very far by buying tickets and turning up with your camera. More and more concert halls are restricting the use of cameras and, even if they weren't, the type of shot you would get from the main floor of the concert hall would probably be useless for publication purposes. Before you can begin to take purposeful pictures of musicians and singers in action, you have to get a press pass which will gain you admittance to the area immediately in front of the stage or to the wings. The best way of getting such a pass is to persuade a local newspaper editor to allow you to cover a concert on the newspaper's behalf. You then have to persuade him or her to apply for a press pass for you. How you persuade the editor is up to you, but the best method is to show your portfolio and ask very nicely. Nine times out of ten you'll be told that a staff photographer will be covering the event and your services won't be required, but you can be almost certain that the staff photographer's pictures will turn out to be poor, and if you keep plugging away, you may get a chance to show what you can do.

The reason that the experienced press photographer's pictures may be poor, is that he or she will be working outside all their normal limitations. Live music photography is one of the hardest of all styles of photography, as it must all be shot under 'available light'. Photographers will know that this means taking

146

pictures using only the light available on stage from the theatrical lights. Local newspaper photographers are often taught that flash is the answer to low-light situations and they find themselves in trouble when they realise that a) flash won't give them a good picture of a distant figure on a stage and b) they're not allowed to use flash close to the artist for fear of upsetting the show. Understanding this, you should be in a better position to get good pictures, but you have to develop a special technique for overcoming the problems.

This is not the right place for a long discourse on the problems of shooting in available light, but in simple terms the technique demands that both black-and-white and colour film are up-rated and that only the finest lenses are used. The cheaper lenses that work perfectly in all normal situations will immediately show their shortcomings when light becomes scarce and apertures widen. Stage lighting appears bright to the audience, but it is very low level for photography, especially for colour photography. With colour, the photographer has the added problem of a mixture of colour temperatures. To get the right facial expression, most pop photographers have to use a long lens (at least 135mm on a 35mm format) and have to work with the aperture wide open — as low as f1.8 where this is available. This aperture asks the utmost of the lens and when that is coupled with the necessity of using very slow shutter speeds — a 30th-of-a-second would be considered fast — the problems are compounded.

The biggest problem, however, is getting the right picture. When I was working as a journalist on a music paper in the early 1970s I developed an interest in photography. As a result, I started to look more critically at the flood of pictures arriving in the *Sounds* office and I slowly developed the egotistical notion that I could do better myself. As a glutton for punishment, I added to my three nights a week concert going by grabbing all of the other press passes that were tossed round the office and turning up at the events with my camera bag. I had made sure I had all the right gear, because I had learned enough about the

147

science to know that an Instamatic with a flash wasn't going to let me beat the experienced pros with whom I jostled for position in the stage wings. Night after night I turned up with my press pass, camera and smile, and the professionals greeted me with generosity. They didn't object when I stood behind them, trying to share their viewpoint. They didn't mind talking to me about their choice of film stock, shutter speeds, processing methods and they passed on a thousand other little tips that they had learned over the years.

I banged away convinced that I was developing a profitable sideline. Over the period of a few months, however, I realised that the few pictures of mine that had been published had probably appeared out of friendship rather than because the picture was deserving of publication. I started re-comparing my work to the work of the professionals and I could see an immediate difference. We had been at the same gig, the same night, standing in the same spot, but whilst my pictures turned out as ordinary, the professionals' pictures had captured a move-ment, an expression or a gesture which had lifted their picture from the mundane to the spectacular and ensured its full page use on the front page of the best papers. I was mystified as to the reason. I remember particularly the generosity of Michael Putland, a photographer who was, even then, a star amongst rock'n'roll photographers and who has since gone on to provide the world with one of the richest libraries of pop photographs. I would stand beside him and shoot the same scene, but his pictures were breathtaking and mine were dull. I realised that he was catching moves and movements I missed. I bought myself a motor drive with the intention of shooting everything. I used up hundreds of rolls of film but, with the exception of a few lucky accidents, my pictures remained dull while his sparkled.

A performance photograph, shot in available light. Being a pop photographer is extremely difficult. This is an example of a photograph too poor to make the grade. Fumble, in action, at a Copenhagen festival in 1973 — in a photograph 'missed' by the author.

When I analysed the difference I realised that being a good pop photographer isn't just a question of owning the right equipment and getting access. Mike, and the few others like him, had the gift of anticipation (and considerable experience) and were able to sense when the opportunity for a good shot was coming. They captured it while I was still lifting the camera. A split second later the moment had passed while I was still fumbling for the button. Added to this gift, Mike and the others had developed superb printing techniques to bring out the maximum possible contrast from thin negatives. Once I recognised my mediocrity as a pop photographer I returned to my amateur status with the consolation that I had, at least, identified the reason for my failure. The amateur photographer who wants to shoot live music must ensure that he or she has this gift. Only by trying will you find out, but without it, you'll get nowhere. The best way of finding out is to ask local bands to allow you to photograph them on small gigs. They'll be only too pleased and you'll develop material for a portfolio which you can show newspaper editors when you are trying to persuade them to get you a press pass to the big gigs. There are no openings for 'assistant live-photographers' so it is a question of going it alone or not going it at all.

Studio photography, whether of rock groups or baked beans, demands money and concentration. It is possible to join a studio photographer as an assistant, but that is a short term occupation and must be regarded as a stepping stone to becoming a solo photographer. A lot of money is needed to set up a studio. It can't be done today on less than £10,000 and it could cost considerably more. Just setting up won't allow you to take good pictures, of course. Just as the live photographer requires the gift of anticipation, so the studio photographer requires the ability to concentrate and go on concentrating. The studio is a controlled environment where the very best possible picture must be produced. This not only means endless work to get the very best lighting, it also means working as hard as possible on the subject to make him, her or them look precisely how they are supposed to look. Shooting usually takes a day, with the first half of the day spent getting the lighting right. Studio photographers do tend to specialise and those who like handling inanimate objects, such as baked bean cans, rarely work with people and vice versa. There are several photographers who make a good living out of photographing pop stars and showbusiness personalities, but it takes an enormous amount of luck to become an assistant in such a studio. The only practical advice that can be given is to write regularly stating precisely why you think you would be a useful assistant.

There are many other jobs which are on the fringes of the music business; some hairdressers work only for music stars and some designers only do stage clothes, but such careers are hard to describe in music business terms, even though the practitioners may have valid reasons for regarding themselves as in the music business. Being in the business is a state of mind: if that's where you want to be, you shouldn't settle for anything less.

APPENDIX

Further Education Courses for Sound Engineers

At the moment there is only one full-time study course for those wishing to become sound engineers. It is run by the University of Surrey and the prospectus can be obtained from

Music Department,
Surrey University,
Guildford,
Surrey.

The course is a four year degree course and during the fourth year the student works in a studio under the Industrial Training Scheme. Like any university, entrance qualifications are strict and include three A levels (maths, physics and music). There are currently eight places on the course each year and in past years about half of these have gone to women.

Association of Professional Recording Studios

Association of Professional Recording Studios,
23 Chestnut Avenue,
Chorleywood,
Herts. WD3 4HA.

READING LIST

UK

Disco International And Club News, monthly, Mountain Lion Productions Ltd, 410 St John Street, London EC1V 4NJ (tel. 01-278 3591).

International Musician & Recording World, monthly, Cover Publications Ltd, 141-143 Drury Lane, London WC2 (tel. 01-379 6342).

Melody Maker, weekly, IPC Specialist and Professional Press Ltd, Surrey House, 1 Throwley Way, Sutton, Surrey SM1 4QQ (tel. 01-643 8040).

Music And Video Week, weekly, Spotlight Publications Ltd, 54 Long Acre, Covent Garden, London WC2 (tel. 01-379 3845).

Music Trades International, monthly, Turret Press, 886 High Road, London N12 9SB (tel. 01-446 2411).

Music U.K., monthly, Folly Publications Ltd, 26-28 Addison Road, Bromley, Kent (tel. 01-460 9679).

Music World, monthly, Columbia Communications (UK) Ltd, 42 Rayne Road, Braintree, Essex (tel. 0376 20629).

New Musical Express, weekly, 5-7 Carnaby Street, London W1V 1PG (tel. 01-439 8761).

Sounds, weekly, address as for *Music and Video Week.*

Studio Sound & Broadcast Engineering, monthly, Link House Magazines, Link House, Dingwall Avenue, Croydon CR9 2TA (tel. 01-686 2599).

USA

Billboard, weekly ($2), Billboard Publications, 9000 Sunset Blvd, Los Angeles, California 90069.

Contemporary Keyboard, monthly, GPI Publications, 20605 Lazaneo Drive, Cupertino, California 95014.

DB — The Sound Engineering Magazine, monthly ($3), Sagmore Publishing Co Inc, 1120 Old Court Road, Plainview, Long Island, New York 11803.

Down Beat, monthly, Maher Publications, 222 West Adams St, Chicago, Illinois 60606.

Guitar Player, monthly, address as for *Contemporary Keyboard*.

Journal Of The Audio Engineering Society, 8 times annually ($10), AES Inc, 60 E 42nd St, New York.

Modern Recording, monthly, Cowan Publishing Corp, 14 Vanderventer Ave, Port Washington, New York 11050.

Music & Sound Output, bi-monthly, Output International Publications Inc, 220 Westbury Avenue, Carle Place, New York 11514.

International Musician And Record World, monthly, International Musician and Recording World Ltd, 12 West 32nd St, 3rd Floor, New York City, New York 10001.

Record World, weekly ($2), Record World Publishing Inc, 1700 Broadway, New York, 10019.

INDEX